TRICK

OF THE

PORCH

LIGHT

TRICK
OF THE
PORCH
LIGHT

JESSICA BARKSDALE INCLÁN

M UTHFEEL PRESS

Contents

TRICK

OF THE

PORCH LIGHT

Trick of the Porch Light

Higgins lived with his mother, but then she died. Higgins now in charge, her house smells like dry things. Paper and wind. Coffee like brittle green leaves, as if he's making tea. Periodically, he opens the door and calls for Calla, his old calico. His voice sounds like gravel under spinning tires. Like he yells a lot, but in all my knowing of him, Higgins has never yelled once, not even at the cat.

We sit in his living room, me reading his journal. His short stories are like haunted houses. Dark window eyes and peeling paint. Squeaky plank porches. There's that screen door on rusty hinges. Bang! No lights, of course. Telephone wire cut. Formerly dead person now ghost at the top of the stairwell holding an axe. Things will not go as planned.

And they haven't, at least for me. Higgins is the backup to my backup plan. The stay at my mom's fizzled. All my other friends had turned into or were Marco's friends, too. They know what I did to him. So I ended up here at Higgins' house, slightly preserved, circa 1992, white counters and appliances, electric range with black saucer burners. Lots of rose and gray upholstery, walls festooned with farmhouse designed borders: chickens, eggs, barns, sunrises with pointy yellow suns.

I met Mark Higgins in kindergarten. We called him Tiny instead of Mark because he was, slight and reedy with leprechaun ears and thin hair. Now he's twenty years older but not much bigger, though no one calls him Tiny anymore, much less Mark. Just Higgins.

"What?" I say, feeling his owl eyes.

"You're a slow reader."

"You've been saying that since seventh-grade English."

"Still true."

"I'm *still* reading," I say.

"Do you like it?" His eyes are round, dark, and deep, black as the inside of something no one should ever see. His hipster beard thin, patches of skin like reverse leopard spots.

"I'm only halfway through," I say. "Can't make a statement yet."

"What's happening?" Higgins leans forward.

"Hard to say." I close the journal. "We're in a house. There are a couple of creepy characters. Plus that narrator. I'm not sure about him."

Higgins sits back against the couch upholstered with roses or chrysanthemums. "You like it?"

"I didn't say that yet."

"But you will."

Outside, a car starts. So do I.

"Chill," Higgins says.

My heart doesn't agree. My heart doesn't agree with me, either. What am I doing here away from Marco and his casseroles and pot plant factory in the back bedrooms? Away from my mother and her hairspray and little dogs. Away from my formerly adequate string of retail jobs. Hiding out in Higgins' house, hoping the cops don't come looking for me.

"No one knows you're here," Higgins says. He clicks on the baseball game. The Giants are winning. Higgins grabs a handful of popcorn.

I go back to reading.

Tuna and green bean. Chicken and dumplings. Beef and barley. Tofu and something peanut. In a pan. In a crock pot, simmering all day long, the kitchen thick with spices. Chopped onions sautéing in a cast-iron pan. Mounds of garlic, green bell peppers, carrots, snow and sugar peas. Chunks of chorizo, mounds of sausage, strips of bacon. Slabs of steak and pork and ribs. Flames and hot, crackling fat. Thyme, basil, oregano. Cooking shows on 24/7, Marco pausing the show to stir the veg or check on the humidity in the back rooms. Coming back with a joint tucked into the corner of his mouth. Wafts of smoke so dense I'm high just from breathing. So high I don't do much more than read magazines at the kitchen table, drink green tea, learn how to cut an onion like a pro.

Days and nights of cooking and eating and smoking, so many I forgot to enroll at the community college or get a temp job that would lead to bigger and better things these jobs always promise.

From Marco and his cooking to Higgins and his short story. My fabulous options.

"You should go in, you know. For a scan or tests or whatever they do." Higgins passes me the box of cereal, the same kind we ate for breakfast before he headed out to the old folk's home where he works. English major. He teaches them how to write about the lives they still remember. After that, he runs a needle at a tattoo parlor on Telegraph Avenue, though his own skin is white and pale and untouched.

I look down at the soggy oats floating in the milk. I can't even bear to think about the orange juice container. Homeless, jobless, mostly friendless, I've accomplished most of the known mistakes (not going to college, staying with the wrong man, living a life of near crime) and now I am going to bring in another person to this festival of delights. Add it to the list.

"I don't know what's going on in your story," I say, rather than answer him about the tests. "It's in parts. One minute we're in the living room. The next in the past. Back at his grandmother's house. How did that happen?"

Higgins chews. "Magical realism."

I pause. "What's that?"

"When magic exists with the ordinary. Talking mirrors. Headless horsemen. Girls who turn into spiders. Ghosts who like bedside chats."

"There's nothing weirder than reality in your story."

"Not yet," says Higgins. He pushes his glasses up his nose and sits back against his chair. He's wearing an old blackish t-shirt from some decade we barely lived through. Tom Petty and the Heartbreakers, though Heartbreakers is missing three Es and a K.

"I'm deep in the conflict," I say. "You can't bring in a ghost now."

"Not a ghost, maybe. But something. You'll see."

I swallow, forcing the cereal to stay in my stomach. Higgins chews, the sound of his staying alive the worst sound ever. Here we are, pushing stuff inside ourselves so we don't die. What's the point? And how much work. Every day, over and over again, and then for what? We're still here and shitting everywhere. Marco's specially prepared meals ended up the same as this cereal, of which Higgins needs to get more so we can keep on living for a few more days.

Suddenly, I long for my mother, forgetting that I didn't long for her when I lived with her. Not once, except if longing can be in reverse, me wanting her to go away. Like Jamaica or Peru. But now all I want is to breathe in her cigarette breath and smell her Diet Coke and rum on ice. How many drinks did I hand her from the minute I learned to pour? Right now, my hands curl into the memory of a tall drink glass. My foot readies to kick away my mother's mutts, Corkie, Phoebe, Tootsie, Palmer, Gorgeous, fuzzy little shits barking up my leg.

I hated those times, and now ten years later, I want to go back.

Maybe if I time-traveled, I'd figure out how to change it, her, everything. I'd make her be a parent who cared so that I would. I'd go to college. I'd get a good job. At this great job and because of my brilliance at doing something important, I'd attract the attention of an even more brilliant man. Brilliant and handsome. Then, boom! A happy life. I'd never be the girl who bounced around the mall, finally ending up at Williams-Sonoma, where Marco found me the day he needed to buy a pasta wheel and a 4-quart sauce pan.

"Don't cry," Higgins says now. "It's going to be okay."

He gets up and hands me a paper towel so thick it feels almost like cardboard.

"Is it?" I ask. "Really?"

"I'll take you," he says. "Dress you up in a clown costume. It's almost Halloween."

"Being pregnant feels like constant Halloween," I say, though really, Higgins' plan is the best I've heard in weeks.

The nurse pushes up my clown outfit, though it's not just a clown outfit but "sexy clown" with garters. I didn't bother with those, the red thigh-highs, or the cute button clown nose, but I do have on the red wig and the striped blouse.

"Cute," the receptionist said when I checked in.

The wig itches, the clown blouse sleeves pinch. Before we left the house, Higgins painted my mouth red, my eyes white, a big black tear on my left cheek.

"Why do you have this thing hanging around?" I asked.

"Just in case."

"Of what? A gender-bending Halloween? A random girl victim to kidnap and dress up?"

Higgins blushed and started to hum *Tears of a Clown.*

"Don't you dare," I told him. "Don't sing that song. I mean it!"

He put down his mother's old eyebrow pencil, and I had half a mind to pick it up and draw a spider on his nose. He crooned in his light, clear voice:

But in my lonely room I cry

the tears of a clown

when there's no one around

"Bastard," I said, yanking on my wig.

Now, the nurse measures my belly with a yellow measuring tape. I stare at the ceiling, wondering why no one ever puts up signs on clinic room ceilings.

Cheer up! It could be worse!

At least you have insurance!

At least you could get insurance!

Too bad your baby daddy's in jail!

Better luck next time!

"It's been a while since you've been in to see us," the nurse says, jotting down my stomach's prodigious growth.

"Three months," I say. "I was away."

She doesn't look at me, sexy pregnant clown girl that I am. "The baby is developing well. Everything's fine. Due date December 1."

She finally glances up from her notes. In her gaze, a pool of world-weariness due to the uninformed yet still reproducing. "We have prep classes. Every Wednesday night. You start next week, and you can get at least four in before baby comes."

Baby. She hands me a pamphlet. *Labor Day Hints. Bringing Home Baby. Breastfeeding 101. Diapers—Cloth or Disposable? Baby's First Shots: Health Facts and Fiction.*

"Are you all set up?"

"Mostly," I lie, pulling my clown shirt over my stomach.

"Do you work at a daycare?" she says.

"Why do you ask that?" I wonder if I look like a person who

could care for anyone or anything other than herself. A person with some substance. Someone you could trust. Someone you would leave your children with all day long without a second thought.

She smiles for the first time. "The clown costume? I bet you forgot you were even wearing it."

The baby is up all night. Moving her fingers and toes. Under my skin, stretching toward life. I get out of bed and read Higgins' journal on the couch. I've not made much progress, and I think he keeps writing it so I have something to do. The narrator in Higgins' story is probably crazy, holed up with a guy he met at a bar. They've had some pretty angry sex. There was a murder, too, a woman who supposedly slipped down the stairs. Socks. Basket. That kind of thing. But the woman's head wounds were incompatible with her husband's story. Police think hammer, hoe, drain pipe. No murder weapon has been found. Yet.

I sip my glass of now-warm milk. I know a little about crime because of Marco. That last night, we went to bed as usual, alarm set so he could wake up and turn on the heat at some crucial budding phase. The next thing I knew, Marco's hand covered my mouth.

"Quiet," he whispered, slipping out of bed.

At first, I thought it was my heart pounding, but then I knew it was the baby telling me something with her whole body. I got out of bed and put on my shoes. While Marco headed toward the back rooms, I slipped down the hall toward the kitchen, grabbing things as I did. Purse. Sweater. Keys. A stack of hundreds in the kitchen junk drawer. I was sweating and praying, and then I saw lights go on. Flash. A crack of window glass. Swearing. Thumping against walls. Then lots of yelling.

Marco always said, "If someone finds me, it's not going to be good. Guns and shit."

"But pot's legal now," I reminded him the first time.

"Kind of," he said.

Outside, I thought to turn back. But instead, I called 911.

"Burglary," I said and gave the woman our address. "Maybe worse."

Ten minutes later, I was on the highway. The tank was full, so I headed to my mother's house and all her disappointment and smelly dogs.

"Cops told me about an informant. Female, they said. Who else could it have been? Shit, after all I fed you," Marco said when he finally called from Santa Rita, charged with gun possession and possession of a prohibited weapon, those nunchuks in the kitchen drawer. "That steak. The pies."

"I'm sorry," I said.

"Not yet you aren't." And then he hung up.

Higgins' fictional murderer is in Santa Rita jail. Part of me wishes he is real. Part of me wishes he is Marco's cellmate. Because Marco won't ever believe I made the call to save him.

"No problem," I imagine him saying with a snap of his fingers. "I could've taken them, like that."

After another five minutes, the baby spins herself down into the nest of my hips, bones like a crown around her soft head. I can imagine her, eyes closed, arms crossed, knees up and tucked. I turn off the light and go back to bed.

Higgins sets up the crib. His sister gave it to him, along with a baby bathtub, some clothes, a changing table, and a car seat.

"She was all, 'God, I'm never having another. Let Amber keep all this stuff for life.' So here it is."

"You told her I was here?" I say, feeling places in my body where air should have been. "That I was pregnant?"

Higgins blushes like a firewall. Fast, all at once, red. "Who does Karen know, anyway?"

I lean against the wall and watch him set up the crib, Calla winding around my legs. Who did Karen know? She was almost 12 years older than us, in her late thirties. Higgins had been a "surprise" baby, as Mrs. Higgins used to say. So Karen probably didn't know Marco or any of his "associates." The last time I saw Karen was at Higgins' and my high school graduation. She looked like her mom had when I'd met Higgins. She and her husband were shortish and slightly lumpy. Their toddler sat like a potato in her dad's arms, the other two were running around on the football field shrieking. I can only hope the crib isn't contagious.

"You're right," I say. "That's really nice of her."

Later, Higgins served up some soup he'd bought. "It's got spinach in it," he says now, handing me a bowl of hotness that swirls with vegetables. "That's important."

I start eating, only caring that it's not cereal. "It's good," I say.

"And stuff like that is better for the baby." He sits down with a bowl but doesn't eat. I swallow, wipe my mouth, glance at him. He's slightly sweaty, glowing, his thin hair sticking up straight, his glasses pressed against his nose for a change.

"What?" I ask.

"Aren't you excited?" he asks.

"About the soup?" I swallow another spoonful and then another, suddenly ravenous. He pushes some bread toward me, and I eat one piece and another, smearing butter over each slice. I can't stop, draining the soup bowl and then taking Higgins' bowl, too. It's like I can finally taste stuff, even if it's overcooked spinach, canned tomatoes, mushy chickpeas. He sits back and watches until I'm done.

"Are you?"

"Huh?"

"The baby. Excited."

On command, the baby kicks, spins inside me like a cog in a machine, her six o'clock gyration. "Not really. But not unexcited."

Higgins beams, stands up, and gets me another bowl of soup.

That night, Calla and Higgins slip into bed with me. Calla, I get. Higgins? It's been two months of me hiding out at his house, after all.

It gives me the creeps, though, his arm around me. Yeah, we used to spoon like this when we were kids, one of us upset about something huge. You know, what gets us all upset: parents' horrible remarks, being teased, being rejected by the most beautiful guy in school. Or in Higgins' case, bullied. Pushed around, beat up, smashed in the mud. But we were officially older now. People who should be sleeping with other people.

But what can I say? He feeds me and got me a crib. He literally butters my bread.

I wait for his next move. Breast. Ass. But it's stomach. Baby, actually. He rubs in slow circles from my lower abdomen up to just above my belly button, his hand warm and dry and gentle. The baby spins her little spin. Elbow. Knee. Foot.

Marco used to flip me over like a griddlecake and munch his way down my middle. He'd whap me around to the other and ride me from behind. He'd slap me on top of him and make me gallop him all the way home.

Higgins doesn't seem to want more. But, I think as I fall asleep, is there anything that easy from anyone?

The baby kicks. Calla purrs. Higgins snores. I blink into the dim light of the bedroom and wait. Higgins pulls me close.

Even though Higgins turned off the porch light and didn't carve a pumpkin, the doorbell starts ringing at about five p.m. It's not even dark yet. The kids stomp down the path and scream, parents waiting up on the street, chatting and drinking out of red plastic cups. The night sky bears down, hugging the streetlight. The neighborhood was closed off at about four with yellow police tape, and now, the whole street vibrates with noise. Calla has slipped under the house.

Earlier, Higgins told me to put on the clown outfit.

"Just in case. And if anyone asks, you're my cousin," he said as he filled a metal bowl with Dumdums and KitKats.

"You're prepared," I said.

"I hate it when I don't have candy." He put the bowl on a chair by the door. "It's wrong. Can't stand their disappointed faces."

So now I sit at the dining room table, finishing Higgins' story and listening to him say, "And what are you? Elsa? From *Frozen*? And you? A little NASA dude?"

I nod to their high-pitched answers, my clown hair bobbing. In the story, the murderer sits in his cell. Back at the murder house, one character plots another murder. That's one busy house. After a half-hour, Higgins comes into the dining room, the bowl empty.

"I have to go to the store." He walks into the kitchen and rummages in the cupboards.

He comes back into the dining room, carrying a yellow bag of chocolate chips. In high school, they were a staple, what we used to make cookies with after smoking a joint. Marco never stooped so low. His chips were always from France, slick, dark, and smooth, melting into perfect shine on the copper double-boiler. Everything he did was the opposite of what I grew up with. Even his food was mysterious, new, maybe even dangerous.

"Give them these if they come to the door."

"Their parents will think I'm trying to poison them."

"Just don't," Higgins says with a flick of a smile. "Do you need anything?"

"I'm good."

Then he's out the door to the garage. I hear the car start, the garage door bang down shut.

No one rings the bell, but I pour the chocolate chips into a small bowl, just in case. But even my mother would have made me throw them out if I returned with this after trick-or-treating.

"God damn cyanide," she would have said. "Sick bastards."

I go back to reading Higgins' story. It's the narrator's and his lover's last night in the murder house. He knows that his lover is going to do something bad. That's how he rolls, this guy. He probably killed someone before they got to the house, and he seemed to be wanting to kill someone after. The narrator's attracted to all his sickness, but he's tired of it, too.

Of course—and I'll tell Higgins this later—he should have thought about this murder issue earlier. Maybe in the first paragraph. No one's going to read this story and not say that. But, like most of us, Higgins' character is messed up, confused, sad. He doesn't know who he can really trust. And I guess when that happens, one reaction is to kill whoever is in your way.

I snort, sit back in my chair, strain to hear some kids coming down the path. But it's quiet out there, as if Halloween was cancelled. I close the journal, push it to the middle of the table.

When I met Marco, I thought he was the one I could be with. I spotted him as he scanned the utensils. He found his pasta wheel, spun, and yes, from across the room our eyes met. Sad but true. Next thing, I was at his place all the time, working in the back rooms, trimming the plants, eating, smoking. Having a lot of clearly unprotected sex. The good news is that I only have a baby to show for that questionable behavior.

But mostly, questionable is all I know. People did one thing, and the next you knew, the windows were being bashed in. There you'd be driving into downtown Oakland wearing a clown costume. My baby wouldn't know who her father is or maybe who I am, red-haired and all. The way things were going, I'd end up in labor wearing this very outfit.

Marco would want me to testify. To make me say what he wants me to say. I'd never be able to leave after that. Not with the baby. The ongoing legal case. His sudden poverty. His inability to cook anything.

"Escape hatch," he once said. "Your mom's house. Get rid of those fucking dogs first."

The past week as Higgins spooned me all night, his hand didn't move from my belly. I always knew he was good. I should have seen it back in school. But like his poor character trapped in the murder house, I wanted more.

Higgins has a crib. Soup. A place where, after Marco forgot about me, I might be safe.

The doorbell rings, once, twice. A kick of gravel. A shuffle. Giggling? Kids pulling a prank? A trick? I stand, stretch a little, a hand to my sore back. The baby kicks. I pick up the bowl of chocolate chips and head to the door.

"I promise they aren't poison," I will say.

But it's too late. Everything is poison, and I know that when I open the door. Marco, not in costume, but just as scary as if he were Death carrying his scythe. He's thinner, his hair cropped close. For the first time, his cheekbones slash sharp ridges across his face. His hands are huge, pale, white, and I imagine them around my neck. For our entire relationship, he'd been high, but now he's awake and wicked, dark eyes black in the porch light.

"Trick or treat," he says.

Escape Room

Without consulting her, Miranda's sister signed them up for "Sherlock Holmes: The Cast of the Baker Street Five."

It wasn't Miranda's first choice for an escape room—or an adventure—but she'd been too busy at work to care. Her sister Jilly was adamant that they not do the bank heist or the pirate escape.

"I won't wear an eyepatch," she kept saying. "I really won't. And who uses currency these days, anyway? What's in the vault? Old plates and broken radios?"

If Miranda were trapped in a room and forced to escape in less than sixty minutes, she might as well channel a great detective. Maybe the employees would hand out pipes and funny hats and basset hounds. Did Sherlock Holmes wear a monocle? Maybe she would be able to exclaim *Elementary* and *The game's afoot.*

Plus, she liked the company's tagline and logo: *Can You Escape?*

Today at work, Miranda let the myriad data processes run and close, everything successful. She turned in the code, alerted her project manager, and left her office on Webster Street, driving over the bridge to the city from Oakland, a reverse commute, the second reason she said yes to this ridiculousness. The first reason was because Jilly seemed on edge, ready for another manic episode.

Miranda needed to see for herself before doing an intervention. She was good at them by now. She could spot trouble a mile away.

There was a slight clog before the Fremont Exit, so she hung on the Bay Bridge as the cars crept forward, looking down onto the city, a steeliness despite the afternoon sun. She'd been listening to NPR, but the monotone of voices was too lulling, so instead she turned everything off and opened her window, letting in a light, noisy breeze.

"Oh, my god!" Jilly had said on the phone on Monday. "You won't believe how totally fun it is. We have to do it. I'll bring Zenda."

Jilly was five years younger than Miranda, but always seemed younger than thirty, the exact same person she'd been at fifteen. She was always with a best friend, this one now Zenda, a made up name, or at least that's what Miranda thought. Miranda wasn't exactly sure how Jilly was making her living, though she imagined it was a pastiche of server, Uber-driver, caterer, and jobber this-and-that: food delivery, house-sitting, dog-walking. Jilly had dropped out of college during an especially bad manic swing and never gone back. She lived with a merry-go-round of friends who fell away after a crisis.

The traffic began to move, and Miranda's phone rang. Jilly was probably cancelling at the last moment, as she so often did, no matter the formality of occasion: wedding, graduation, or funeral, especially funerals.

"Miranda Pearson?"

"This is she." Miranda braked for a woman driving a Volvo who decided lanes didn't matter.

"This is Brenda McLean from radiology at Kaiser."

Miranda gripped the wheel. Right. The mammogram. The one her doctor told her to have years before.

"Yes."

"The radiologist wants you to come back for another mammogram," Brenda said.

Miranda wanted to ask why, but why? It was obvious. There was something wrong or something inclusive. There was a blur, a mass, a knob of death, shadow, a tumor, a terrible mystery.

She didn't have to be Sherlock Holmes to deduce that. Besides, no one ever asked you to do something awful twice for fun.

Her heart beat louder than the traffic passing outside her window. Behind her, another motorist honked. Miranda stepped on the gas, made her way off the bridge.

"Ms. Pearson?" Brenda asked.

"I'm here," Miranda said, bearing left toward Market Street. She took the first left, and then turned left again.

"Does next Wednesday at noon work?"

"Of course." She worked at home on Wednesdays. No one would ever know.

"We'll see you on the 16th at noon. Remember, no deodorant or lotion. No powder."

Miranda hung up and stared into the red light. Ahead of her, the sun squeezed through the financial district like a laser. Somewhere, close by, there was a mystery to solve.

"You're late!" Jilly said. "You're never late."

Jilly leaned over for a kiss, and Miranda tried to not breathe in her scent, which was usually part Sauvignon Blanc and a perfume that smelled like spun sugar and something very purple. Today she just smelled like a Fruit Roll-Up.

"Traffic." Miranda noted Jilly's very short skirt and big, black boots. Her hair was straight, long, and dark, a twist of magenta framing the left side of her face.

Jilly handed Miranda a clipboard, a pen dangling from a neon-green chain. Behind her sister stood a dark-haired woman nodding to music coming through earbuds, the kind without wires. Her bangs looked like a perfectly hemmed pencil skirt that rested against her smooth forehead. She wore cat glasses and a short skirt. Both she and Jilly were case studies for planned disorder, a chaos of cool.

"This is Zenda!"

Miranda started to say something but was interrupted.

"Are you ready?" A female employee wearing a red shirt and a houndstooth cap came up and collected Miranda's clipboard. Her curly brown hair fanned out from beneath the hat.

"Looks good!" She was chipper, her voice a small, finely wrought saw. Miranda tried to smile, but the beginning of a headache pulsed behind her eyes.

"Do you need a Coke?" Jilly leaned in. "I can tell. You need a Coke."

"Everyone needs a Coke." Zenda's bangs didn't move even when she nodded.

"Is your name really Zenda?" Miranda asked.

"No refreshments in the escape room," the employee said in the same high voice.

Jilly pressed two pills into Miranda's hand as they walked down the hallway. "Better than Excedrin," she whispered. Jilly and Miranda knew Excedrin, their mother's favorite drug because she refused anything stronger.

"It gives me that extra zing," she always said.

"You have sixty minutes," the employee said. "You may not use cell phones in the room for calls or web search. No photos, please."

"No Google!" Zenda moaned. "I can't do anything without it."

"Have fun," the employee said.

Jilly grabbed Miranda's arm. "This is going to be great."

Anything Jilly said would be great usually ended up a disaster. But hadn't Miranda always been here anyway? She nodded, popped the pills into her mouth, and swallowed. They weren't even remotely Excedrin.

"Your time starts now!"

The employee handed Jilly an instruction sheet, and then let them in and whoosh, the door closed behind them.

The room was decorated like a cheap Edwardian set, the kind from the plays Miranda used to perform in during high school. The walls were covered in a dark paisley wallpaper, and two candelabra-type lighting fixtures hung from the wall. The furniture was wicker with floral cushions or wingback with thick upholstered arms. The carpet was maroon, and a fake fire flickered in the fake fireplace. A set from something Oscar Wilde, maybe *The Importance of Being Earnest*? Or was that Victorian? She didn't know anymore, her whole life devoted to data retrieval and code. She went to work for ten hours a day and then at night, she dreamed of code.

How had that happened?

Zenda bounced around Jilly. "Read it!"

"Is your name actually Zelda?" Miranda asked. "I've never heard of Zenda."

"My mom was totally into her meditation practice," Zenda said. "If I was a boy, she was going to name me Zen."

"Oh." Miranda thought Zen Buddhism was about detaching, and naming a child after a practice seemed to label the child: Look at how special my parents are. Total attachment.

Zenda studied her. "She's Chinese."

The name seemed more aging-white-hippie than Chinese.

"Okay," Jilly said, the instructions open in front of her. "Any good detective must identify the suspects. The Baker Street was a gang of five. Their names are in pieces around the room."

"Pieces?" Miranda's empty stomach gurgled with drugs.

Jilly glanced at the small table near the door. "A puzzle! Look!" She held up a large wood puzzle piece. "Gather! Hurry!"

Her head a whirl, Miranda walked around the room. All around the edges, the real room showed: a heating vent, a green exit sign, a light fixture from the twenty-first century. The air was stale and smelled like imaginary cigars.

Her eyes peeled like a great detective's would be, Miranda found one puzzle piece on the fake mantel and another in the whisk broom by the fireplace. She put them in one hand and her body shook.

Her name meant miracle, which was total overkill on their mother's part. And the only miracle Miranda had ever performed was living through Jilly's young adulthood. Maybe paying rent in the Bay Area was a miracle, too. But the rest of her life had been ordinary. She should have been named Ann or Kay or Lee, perfect middle names that never distracted.

She could use a miracle right about now, one that sounded like, "We made a mistake. Not your mammogram. We are so sorry."

Miranda wanted to look at her phone to see if anyone left such a message, but then she remembered she'd turned off her electronics as per the instructions.

She found another puzzle piece by the lamp. One more by the fake matchbook. As she bent over to pick up the piece, her head pounded, but not as intensely as before. The lights in the room seemed to glow a little purple, green.

"Okay! How many do you have?" Jilly called.

"Four," Miranda said.

"Seven," said Zenda.

"I have ten!" Jilly said, her voice shrill. "Come on! Let's put it together!"

They dropped their pieces on a small table by the fireplace, and Jilly put the puzzle together in about five seconds. Her fingers were slim and quick.

"A piano player," their mother always said. "Or a pickpocket."

Jilly stood. "Look at the names of the suspects. And this clue. Look at it. Take a picture."

"We can't do that," Zenda said. "Anyway, the puzzle is right here. We aren't going anywhere for another fifty-four minutes."

"What's the next clue?" Miranda asked.

Zenda, hands on her hips, bent over the puzzle, and read: "Pipes are not just for water."

On the wall next to Jilly were shelves, each with a pipe, some made of wood, one that seemed made of clay, one that was large-bowled and swooped.

Jilly squealed and ran over to the display, her hands on the wall until she found something. "A door!"

She pulled open the door, revealing another set of Edwardian mishmash. "Come on!"

Miranda wanted to pull her sister to her and calm her. She needed to wrest the instructions away from Jilly, find the murderer, get into the next room, and then the next and get out of this stupid game and never come back.

But suddenly, the room seemed to lose weight. Even the air on Miranda's skin seemed less than, barely there.

"Oh," she murmured. Her headache was totally gone.

She followed Jilly, agreed to the plan of action—a missing key, a new lead, a true suspect. The key led to a box, the box held some Morse code. Zenda found a code book, and Miranda heard herself reading out the meanings to Jilly who jotted them down on a conveniently located chalk board.

"We're going to find out! This will solve everything!" Jilly cried, her eyes cracked, glittery as broken car window glass on asphalt.

As Miranda followed her sister and Zenda, who, Miranda saw now was not just a friend to Jilly, but more (hand on Jilly's waist, smiles, warm looks), Miranda floated up in the room, hovering over the game, their three bodies and the chintzy sets. She lifted out of the building, over Market Street, high over the bridge, bridges, entire city, the Bay Area, California, the United States, continent.

Sure, she was moving into another room, about to solve the crime, but she was really up, up, up, back to a place of beginning before any of the bad things happened. And then she was so high, all was dark. No moon, no stars, nothing.

When their mother was in the hospital the final time, Jilly was on an upswing, the point just before the swing broke and threw its occupant off into the compacted sand below. Hovering under mania, Jilly had talked to all their mother's doctors, taken notes, called specialists, arranged for home health aides. She'd cleaned, washed, shined. She arrived to the hospital with flowers for their mother and freshly baked cookies for the nursing staff.

Meanwhile, their mother had folded up like a clean table napkin. She was ready to go. Only Jilly hadn't noticed. Or had and refused to see.

Miranda had rushed to the hospital that time, cutting out on her last classes before spring break. She was in her last year of grad school, a data science program.

"You're a woman in tech," her advisor, a woman, had said. "They'll hire you for the novelty alone."

Jilly had just started at the community college and lived at home in her childhood room, at least when she wasn't in rehab or lockdown.

"Don't let her go," their mother had said.

Miranda hadn't been sure what her mother was talking about; she assumed it was all the morphine the hospice nurses were giving her. But when she stopped breathing and her heart gave out, Miranda understood. Jilly was gone. And was for five months, missing the funeral, the paperwork, the selling, the packing.

Miranda worked with the local police department and even hired a private detective. Her friend Susie contacted a psychic who told Miranda that her sister was in a European city living in a wooden structure by the water. Lake or ocean, Miranda wanted to know, but the spirits weren't specific.

In fact, Jilly was by the water and in a wooden structure, but not in Amsterdam or Capri but in a squat in Oakland. She was smoking and taking drugs, eating days-old bread out of dumpsters, and stealing from stores. The private detective found her through a stolen credit card and a camera at a convenience store on Telegraph. Then there was the legal wrangling and a year of putting her back together, enough so that she was able to live in the outside world.

Point was, Miranda could never tell Jilly about the bad mammogram.

The employee with the raspy voice stared down at Miranda intently. Miranda blinked, breathed in the woman's candy flavor and looked up into her pin-sized nostrils. How did she ever survive a cold?

"She's okay," the employee called.

"Too late," someone else said. "Paramedics are here."

Turning, Miranda saw Jilly next to her and then felt her hand in hers.

"I'm sorry," Jilly said. "I shouldn't have given you pills on an—"

Zenda nudged her.

"I'm sorry," Jilly continued. "Oh, Mirry."

"Worse than those mushrooms," Miranda said, amazed by Jilly's use of Mirry, a childhood nickname, one their father had used in the years before he left them all for good.

"Shhh," Jilly said, scooting away as the paramedics bustled in.

"No one's ever fainted in Sherlock," the employee told the first paramedic, a handsome man built like a toy troll, all head and arms.

"It's not very exciting," Jilly agreed. "Too easy."

"She fainted," the employee said, her tone defensive. "Must have done something right."

"I have a migraine," Miranda said. "I'm dehydrated. I'm just fine."

The paramedic nodded at all of them, but he and his partner—a thick, tense woman with black eyes—took her vitals. Blood pressure, pulse, temperature, pupils.

Everything was normal.

They wrapped Miranda in a blanket and sat her on a bench with a large glass of water. Jilly and Zenda took care of the Escape Room paperwork and insurance forms. Meanwhile, the employee hovered, as if making sure none of the papers involved lawsuits, lawyers, litigation.

"I'm fine," Miranda said to everyone who asked because she had to be the one to hold it together. If she hadn't fainted, lord knows what Jilly would be doing now. "Really, I'm just fine."

Statistically, women whose mothers were diagnosed before the age of forty have twice the risk of getting the disease.

Miranda's mother was diagnosed at thirty-eight and spent years trying not to die.

But she had the kind of cancer that most didn't survive.

"Watch yourselves," their mother's doctor told Miranda at the funeral, the one without Jilly. "Zoe was an amazing woman. She wouldn't want either of you to suffer."

Miranda was never sure what that meant. Should she and Jilly kill themselves to avoid a death like their mother's? Was that what the doctor was trying to say? Their sudden and eventual death was inevitable, unavoidable, and imminent? Later, various doctors told her she could have genetic testing and then a prophylactic double mastectomy. She could have her ovaries removed, too, and then she could roam the planet denuded of primary and secondary sex characteristics.

No wonder Jilly ran away.

"Okay, sweetie. Arm up." The technician lifted Miranda's arm and shoved one small breast under the plastic plate. "Too tight? No? Okay."

She walked behind the screen. "Breathe in, don't exhale."

The machine hummed and then stopped. "Exhale. Relax. Okay, that's it."

She came back around and smiled as she unhinged Miranda from the machine. Sweaty and slightly shaking, Miranda peeled herself off and stepped back, trying to avoid the screen at the back of the room where she saw her breasts in digital black and white. Whatever would kill her was in this room right now.

"I've sent the images to the radiologist on-call. So if you want to wait here, you can."

Miranda nodded because she couldn't speak. She picked up her bra, which seemed ludicrous now, small cups of fabric to hold lumps of flesh that no one wanted her to have. Inside each, ounces of death.

The technician turned on the lights, flicked off the screen, closed her computer, and indicated a strange couch in the room, as if something in a slipcover might keep patients from forgetting the point of the entire space.

Miranda sat, unable to use her phone. A sign that hung over a white cabinet told her not to. Instead, she picked up an old *Wom-*

an's Day magazine, full of articles about home gardens and children's lunches.

She flicked through the pages, all the women and children happy in article and ad alike. There was a diversity of people in the pages, but all of them were living the same happy life in television-set towns and perfect, first-world houses. Not even a ghost of her childhood showed up in this magazine. Their mother was like her name, exotic and different. They never ate carrot sticks with peanut butter only with humus; apples weren't sliced but cut up with cucumbers in a vinaigrette. Their garden featured heirloom vegetables and a pot plant—a large, almost pine tree-looking growth with dark, resinous buds.

Both she and Jilly were allowed to dye colored streaks in their hair and wear mismatched clothes, not that Miranda ever did either. But Jilly had magenta and yellow streaks and wore plaid with swirls and dots. And she learned to clip the buds off the pot plant to dry and later smoke.

Before Miranda put the house on the market, she'd dug up the plant and given it to one of Zoe's cancer friends. Pot wasn't legal then, so the plant had come in handy for brownies, cookies, and candy that Zoe ate for years to quell her nausea.

"Ms. Pearson." Miranda put down the magazine and stood, smoothing her blouse, feeling a button in the wrong hole or an unhooked hook in her bra.

"I'm Dr. Poddar. I've looked at your images." She was a tall, slim woman with what looked like red, gold, and blue Christmas tinsel in her hair. Miranda stared at her, amazed by the way the dark room threw light into the doctor's strands, the tinsel twinkling.

"We called you in for another look because one image had a spot that didn't appear elsewhere."

She moved to the machine and clicked, turning the screen a bit for Miranda to see. "But it's not there now. Everything looks just fine." Dr. Poddar nodded, still pointing to a spot now empty of worry. "Do you have any questions?"

Of course she had questions: Are you sure your test is right? It wasn't for my mother. Or, What mistake did you make the first time? And, What if this time was the real mistake?

But these were answers she couldn't hear now. Miranda shook her head.

"Thank you for coming back in. Make sure to always keep your appointments as per your doctor's recommendation."

Dr. Poddar smiled and turned on her heel, leaving Miranda behind with the large machine with its breast-smashing plates.

"Okay, sweetie," the technician said as she bustled back into the room and headed to her computer behind the screen. "You're good to go."

Once she got home, safe and okay and healthy, she couldn't get out of bed. At first, Miranda thought she must have picked up a bug from a doorknob at the hospital, but her entire bodily response had come on too quickly. Her bones ached and her flesh felt weighted down. Her face, hands, and feet tingled. Her stomach roiled.

She managed to email work to say she was taking paid time off for the afternoon, but that afternoon turned into the next day, and the day after that. She didn't answer her calls, stopped looking at email, Skype, Slack, and texts, and turned her face to the wall, her blankets pulled up, her body shivering.

Day turned to night, Friday turned into the weekend. Saturday cracked open like a rotten pumpkin. Her phone rang so often she turned it off, letting it slide somewhere under the bed.

Miranda had only gotten out of bed to pee, drink water, and eat crackers, but hours went by in a haze of potential fever and restless sleep. The room opened up with light and then closed up dark. The air closed in tight, and she practiced not breathing.

In her dream, she was a child and Jilly was holding her in her arms, the way their mother used to hold them and sing. But then it was her mother, just as she remembered her, soft and warm and smiling.

"Mom?" Miranda asked, reaching out for her mother's hair, surprised to find she still had some. She'd come back to life and so had her curls.

"Oh, sweetie," her mom said.

Miranda smiled, her body light now, buoyant with joy. "You came back."

"From where?" Mom said in a voice not hers. "Miranda, wake up. Wake up!"

There was noise, another voice, the sound of windows opening. Someone was shaking Miranda, and she opened her eyes and looked up at her sister. Jilly was leaning over her, her face dark with concern.

"Have you been drinking? Did you take something?"

Miranda struggled out of her sister's arms. "I don't drink. Someone has to stay sober."

"I'm sober," Jilly said.

"You've never been sober."

Jilly's grip tightened. "I've been sober for over a year."

Miranda leaned against the headboard and stared at her little sister. There she was, as always, dressed as if headed to roller derby practice. Short shorts, tank top, hair in a ponytail. But her eyes were clear and sharp and keen, cutting right through Miranda's foggy thoughts.

"But what about those pills you gave me at the escape room?" Miranda's mouth was fuzzy, her words covered in moss.

"That was like a super ibuprofen," said Jilly. "For my cramps."

"But why. . . ?"

"Maybe because you haven't been eating? Zenda looked in the fridge. There's like a stick of butter and a pickle in there."

"Zenda's here?"

"She went to the store. She'll be back." Jilly stood and adjusted the blankets. Her arms were tan and strong, as if she'd been working out.

Noticing her gaze, Jilly nodded. "I know, right? Zenda has me into yoga."

"She's your girlfriend," Miranda said.

"I wondered when you would ask."

Jilly bent down and started picking up clothes, glasses, and wadded up tissues. In a few quick trips, the bedroom was almost clean. In the kitchen, the dishwasher was running. Then, Jilly opened the bedroom window and let in a gust of fresh air, enough to make Miranda wince. She was like their mother, coming into any room and dervishing around.

"The toilet!" Jilly called from the bathroom. "God."

The apartment bloomed with the smell of toilet bowl cleaner.

How long had Jilly been like this? Miranda had missed the clues, all of them right there in front of her, a wooden puzzle she could have put together if she'd only looked for the pieces.

"Don't let her go," their mother had said. Miranda had always supposed their mother wanted Miranda to take care of Jilly. But maybe, all along, she'd known it would come down to this. Jilly was the one who knew how to live.

"I was worried about you," Miranda said when Jilly came back into the room with a bowl of hot soup.

"Why?" Jilly sat on the edge of the bed and patted Miranda's foot.

"I thought you were going on a manic spree."

Jilly shook her head. "I have a new doctor. Things are good."

"Are you sure?"

"There's a difference, you know?"

Was there?

"Eat this terrible soup," Jilly said. "And then Zenda will make you something real."

The soup was hot, the air full of spring, and her sister wasn't crazy.

Jilly sat straight and tall, just as their mother had. She handed Miranda a napkin. "I'm not manic, Mirry. I'm happy."

Miranda nodded and tried to swallow. She wanted to say, "I don't have cancer."

But she didn't want Jilly to know about the almost-cancer. No, she wanted Jilly's happiness to grow and stretch and become what her sister was made of.

Back from the store, Zenda walked into the room and put a hand on Jilly's shoulder, bent down, and whispered something in her ear. They both giggled; something about the dead lettuce in the crisper.

Jilly kept her hand on Miranda's ankle. And soon, Zenda was in the kitchen, moving things around in the cupboards, the air filling with the tang of sautéed onion and garlic. Miranda remembered their early home, their mother concocting crazy dinners with ridiculous ingredients: satsumas, dandelion greens, tofu. Then they would all sit down together, the night filling the sky with questions.

Music wafted into the bedroom with the cooking aromas. Miranda's stomach growled.

"See?" Jilly said.

Murder House

I met Tony Disco on a Saturday night. By Monday, I was confused about a lot of things, but I knew his name was fake, at least the Disco part. After we broke into the house and had eaten two frozen pizzas and some canned ravioli, I used the Wi-Fi to check on Surnames.com. Disco had no known origin. No country. No history. No members claiming Disco as their own.

"You aren't really named Disco," I finally said, as we sat in the living room, the lights out, each of us with our fourth beer. The only sound in the living room was the hum of the great TV, the big black eye hanging on the wall, its blue light blinking.

"No shit, Sherlock," Tony said. He sat head back against the fancy couch, his legs spread, his arms at his sides, one tan hand clutching his beer can. He smelled like the chunky vanilla soap from the shower, his long brown hair in wet perfect curls on his shoulder. One leg pressed against mine, our kneecaps clacking together. I could feel the difference between muscle and bone, the shiver of him still inside me. "Ancestor showed up with a longer name. Greek. Turned it into Disco. Informal like."

I took a big swallow and changed my mind. If a family claimed Disco for decades, I'd give it to them. He reached out for my thigh, his palm straddling my tense muscle.

"What're we gonna do?" I asked.

"We've been doing it, haven't we?" His eyes were black and shiny in the darkened room.

I took another swallow, looked out the window, but, of course, the windows were shut, closed, and covered, the shades drawn tight. The one time I looked out, two old ladies were about to come down the steps. They pointed, made tsk tsks I could almost hear. I wanted to bolt out the door and up the stairs, shooing them away. I had no idea what else Tony Disco would do. I wasn't sure what he'd done to the guy who'd told us both at the bar about the murder and the house no one was in.

"Guy didn't make bail," the dude had said. "Read it in the paper. Police investigation over. Wife dead. Family dead, too. No kids. Just a bunch of crime scene tape and me watching his television and sleeping in his big bed. Asked around. House up in the hills. All those trees and no one paying any attention. Live high on the hog. Whatever's in the fridge, mine, oh mine."

But that guy was gone. In between the fourth and fifth beer at the bar, he disappeared in a haze of yellow and heat. Someone's joke. A crack of broken glass. Tony and the guy out the door. Maybe in the back alley. And then it was all Tony Disco sidling up to me at the bar, his arm warm against mine, his breath like juniper. And now here he and I were, slumped on a dead woman's couch.

So the good news was that the old ladies had turned around and walked away. But I was going to keep an eye out, just the same. One? She reminded me of my grandmother. Short and squat with a bowl of gray hair. The other like my second-grade teacher. Sort of pretty in an old way. Like one of the pressed flowers I used to find in my grandmother's coffee-table books.

"So we've been doing it, right?" Tony repeated, a knife edge in his voice, one finger running up my thigh.

"Guess so."

"Not bad." Tony threw his can across the room. I almost stood to pick it up.

"No," I said instead. It wasn't bad, Tony's long body on the big bed. The empty house. The beer. The respite from wherever it was I'd been doing until I met him at the bar. Living at the squat on East 29th, picking up work at the chocolate factory banging together wooden display shelves, spending my money at bars, drinking beer and throwing darts. The hum of whatever covering up whatever it was that needed covering up. Just like now. Here we were, floating down a river I'd never been on before. I was like the murderer in jail. All new digs. Just like that.

"Let's go back to bed," Tony said.

"Okay," I said, shaking inside from at least two things. "Let's."

Sex with a man is different than with a woman. Yeah, dumbass. Obviously. Right. But I didn't know that before Tony Disco. I was conversant in pussy and mouth. Anyone's mouth. Anyone's drunk bar party fucked-up mouth. Lips and tongue. Pretty universal. Pussy is wet and warm, unending, the tunnel back to the beginning, the start and the finish, slick and expected.

But dick was a language I only knew from experience with my own. Up and down. Hard and soft. I had no idea what Tony would do to me on the bed. I had no idea how it would go. When Tony yanked me close, he might have killed me as much as kissed me, his mouth hard as if he were trying to take something back I'd borrowed and forgotten to return. Something I'd stolen that he needed more than anything. Something important he wanted to fight over. He was wiry and strong, bone and muscle in equal proportion, not one soft place on him. Sex with Tony was hot and sweaty and dirty. Shaming, painful, and amazingly intense. My heart about pounded out of my chest, desire an alien wanting to escape, grow up, and kill everything in sight.

Later, as we lay on the bed stripped bare except for the sheet, lights out, I ruminated. Maybe this was a new lifestyle. I could honestly say I wasn't born to be fucked up the ass. It wasn't an innate need. Probably, I could have walked out of the house and never done it again. But I didn't leave. And we did it again. And again.

"There's two old bitches out there," Tony said from the bedroom.

I was in the bathroom counting my wounds. Two bruised kiss bites on my forearm. A bloody nose. A pucker of purple on my left cheek. My asshole a well of hurt. Scratches on my chest. All my muscles ached from strain.

The beer had run out, and we'd started in on the red wine racked in the basement. My mouth was dry, my eyes burned. The back of my throat rough and red as if I'd been swallowing the front path gravel.

After three days, I needed something green to eat. Spinach or broccoli. Leaves and roots and small roasted animals. The murdered lady had been big into canning things. Jars of fruits, glistening peaches, pears, and plums behind the dusty glass. All that fiber hadn't helped much in the asshole department. Tons of faded green beans and little round pea things. Tan, though. And big, red rounded lumps of beets. But there was frozen steak and quarts of rocky road ice cream. Wine and bourbon and vodka. My body felt lumpy and soft, something deep inside me beaten to pulp.

"They're just neighbors. Walk in the mornings." I'd seen them every day, around this time, about when Tony and I were ready to fall asleep. The bowl-cut lady usually looking down the stairs into the house as if wanting to spot the murderer at home. Catch him herself. But then they moved on.

"They coulda seen something," Tony said, his voice heavy with fatigue and wine.

"There's nothing to see." I wiped the blood off my lip, wincing. The garbage can was lumped with bloody tissue, the floor strewn with wet and bloody towels. "We haven't turned on a light. We haven't played any music. We haven't started the dryer or anything."

"They know. They'll call the cops," Tony said, his voice trailing away.

I walked back into the bedroom, hanging the towel on the door knob. Tony had fallen asleep that second, spread out like a starfish, mouth open, a snore at the back of his throat. He was older than I first thought. In a bar, everyone's younger. But in the lighter gloom of the dark house, I could see the lines on his face, scars from long ago fights, a strand or two of gray at his temples and in his widow's peak. He was the kind of guy I would have avoided anywhere else. Sleek and dangerous and full of a furiosity that lived under his skin.

At the window, I pulled the curtain open a slit and looked out. My heart beating to the hope of no old ladies. And yes. Nothing but trees and sky, fog whirling against the pine branches.

I stretched to look up to the pale sky. No bad things should have happened up here, this land above the flats of Oakland. No woman should have been found at the bottom of the stairs with a blunt force trauma, inconsistent—the guy at the bar told us before Tony made him disappear—with a fall down a flight of wooden stairs. No amount of slippery woolen socks and heavy laundry basket could make those wounds make sense. No, this shaded, dreamy land was the land of school children and smart people. There were tall trees and soft breezes. Garbage wasn't humped at every corner, and the nights weren't filled with men and women roaming or standing on the corners wanting to sell something.

This place was like where I was brought up in the foothills of the Sierras, living at my grandmother's house after my mom dumped me there. Grandma teaching me how to eat with a fork and comb my hair. To close the bathroom door when taking a shit. To read, do math, take a bus and say thank you to others. To press sugar cookies into rounds and bake them until just golden brown. To sleep on clean sheets and wipe my hands on a napkin. From five till fifteen. Until my grandmother died and my cousins finally pushed me out of the house like a foreign pack of slavering wolves.

All freeways headed down the hill. Only the Pacific Ocean kept me from going further. Five years of bouncing around the Bay Area, one place to crash and then the other. One person with a car and an idea and then another.

I turned back to look at Tony. We had three, maybe four days left here. Tops. And just like those final weeks at my grandmother's house, I was again running with wolves.

"Goddammit!" Tony hissed. "That fucking old lady. She won't stop."

I waited till he moved and looked out the bedroom window. She was alone this time, not with the other one. She stood with her hands on her hips, staring down at the house. It was the wrong time, too. Not early morning. But late afternoon.

"I'm going to have to do something about this," Tony said, his voice and breath at my ear.

The day before, I'd entered Tony Disco's name into one of those background check sites, the kind where you can get some information for free. I used his real name, getting it out of him the night before after he drank a bottle of Despotopoulo cabernet.

There he was. Tony Despotopoulo, 36. Tony only had one address, about ten years ago, a place down in the Valley. Tulare. Before I clicked on one page, the site warned me "This Page May Contain Graphic Information." Mostly, I thought they did that so people would click on the page, wanting that graphic view, violence, death, dismemberment.

I clicked. The rap sheet a column long. Started slow, Tony.

Worked up to aggravated assault. A teaser of more bad things to come. And that's when the site wanted their $12.99. So I clicked off.

"She gonna get it, man," he said to me, his hands on my shoulders, his body humming. His hands started moving over me.

I said nothing but leaned back against him, my eye still on the space where the old woman stood. Tony was going to get it, too.

The murderer's wife liked to can things and knit, a thick, long loopy blanket in every room. From the looks of the photos the police hadn't taken for their investigation, she'd grown up in a big family, so it was odd that they were all dead now. She'd been tall, a lady basketball player, but she liked soft things. Silky underwear. Wool coats fluffy as rabbits. Websites said she'd only been 58 when her husband bashed her head in. I found myself looking around the house for the obvious but still hidden murder weapon: iron, skillet, door stop, hammer.

The murderer was a twisted little runt, his combed-over head barely reaching his wife's chin. He wore thick glasses and ugly brown shoes (pretty much in every photo). His hands were big, which was ironic because he was a locksmith. He liked all sorts of nerd shit. Bookcases bending with science fiction. Star Wars posters in the basement. Ugly ass steins from where-the-hell-ever in the den.

Somehow, though, she'd loved him. Even as he started to make his evil plans. Even as she carried the laundry basket down the slick stairs.

By the end, the steaks and the ice cream were gone. We'd even made Bisquick pancakes without eggs or milk (not a good idea) and eaten all the Cream of Wheat. We'd used all the towels and sheets and toilet paper. With the windows closed, the house smelled like a dirty fish tank. It was time to move on, but Tony sat in a chair by the kitchen window, looking out.

"The least we could do is some wash," I said. "Not the dryer. Just the washer. Spin it twice. Let it dry overnight. Get out of here by five am."

"Don't you like how I smell?" Tony asked, his smile lopsided, his teeth gleaming. He'd used up all the woman's special brightening toothpaste.

Did I? Maybe not so much anymore, both of us rank with overuse.

"At least our t-shirts," I said.

"Fine." Tony stood, stretched, a waft of him in my nose. "We can't let the old biddies see us. I'm still not sure they aren't trouble."

"They won't bother you," I said. "They'll just keep walking."

Tony shook his head, the way he had at the bar that night when the dude had said, "No way you coming with me. I found the damn house first."

I started picking up my shirts and underwear. Cotton. They'd be dry by tomorrow morning. By eight, I could be back in the Valley. By twelve, in Los Angeles.

Tony rolled to the edge of the bed, picking up his things. His back a ladder of muscles. For a second, I thought to grab the towels to wash them, too, but the murderer was getting stuff washed at Santa Rita Prison. And the wife? Only god knew about that. Anyway, eventually, someone would come through and worry about this mess. They'd know something was up. Probably the one old lady would call the police. She and her pressed flower friend would stand at the top of the stairs and say, "Can you believe it? Twice? We were standing right here! We should have known."

Then they'd go back to their routine, walking every morning until new people moved in and all of this would just be a good story. Something to think about when they were back in their safe, cozy houses drinking coffee, waiting for the next morning and the next walk.

We walked down the dark hallway. Outside, I heard the first of the crickets.

Tony was ahead of me as we moved down the stairs. I held my dirty clothes to my chest, the pile smelling like this dark, greasy week. I felt the weight of the hammer against my forearms. I stared at Tony's curls, the way they bounced as he walked down one step and then two.

What Glory Chose

Glory and her husband Mark sat together at the table, the light brilliant on the newly painted walls. Since they'd been stuck at home, they'd had everything painted. They took the dogs to the beach for a week at a friend's cabin and came home to all white walls. The rooms glowed.

"We need to look for some art," Mark said. "Get color somewhere. Not that I don't like our choice. It's just a bit spare."

Snowy Sunday. That was the color's name.

Art, Glory thought. She would rather have broccoli. Maybe asparagus. Not canned peas. Outside, late winter winds whirled. It had been three years since the day the governor told them to sequester. Sure, they'd had breaks, weeks, months, when numbers were down, the virus seemingly over. Then somewhere—India, Mongolia, Halifax, a small atoll in the South China Sea—another strain would emerge, ravaging (that was the word) the planet. Everyone needed a booster. Then another booster. Then another vaccine altogether. Then a booster for that, them, all. She and Mark stood in line for each of them, but still, here they were, eating canned peas.

Worse, they couldn't see their children. The two eldest lived in the South and had children, one grandchild unable to be vaccinated due to a childhood cancer. Her younger two—people Glory thought had been reasonable, smart, even—refused the second shot, the first booster. With his spotty internet in his remote, off-grid cabin, she hadn't seen her youngest son's face in two years.

"Okay." Glory sat back.

"Then the floors. We can get them refinished in the spring."

Glory nodded again. Did floors even matter? At every house on their block, their street, probably even their town, white vans festooned with colorful logos hunkered in the driveways: Rawhide Electric, Paul's Plumbing, Leaf and Wind Gutter Service. Backhoes backhoed. Sawzalls sawed. Men scaled roofs, cut down trees, unfurled fresh sod onto waiting soil.

No amount of remodeling could fix the world.

While her husband admired the halo of white around them, Glory slid a pamphlet across the table toward him, this man she'd met her first semester of college. Mark picked it up, his face still as he read, opening one fold and then another. On the front, the image of the facility shone. Finally, he looked up, shaking his head.

"After the floors are done," she began. "I want to do this."

Mark had reacted better than Glory imagined he would, at least once he realized that Glory had enough money to pay for the initial freezing procedure and the fifty years of bodily maintenance.

"You want to be frozen for fifty years." Mark took in a breath. "You want to leave me."

"It's not about that."

He gave her a look, one she knew well. "How can you have stashed away enough to pay for it?"

A history professor with his head down in books and now in Zoom meetings, Mark had never paid attention to her job, the one she'd had until three years ago, the job that had supported the remodeling, vacations, and extras he'd taken for granted. What had he thought she earned as a CEO of a national natural foods company? Her face had been on the metro buses for a time alongside warm, caring quotes the ad agency had parsed from her public statements.

"Good food, good life."

"Helping you and the planet for forty years."

The company had been bought up in the early days of the pandemic by a larger money-making animal that began eating its way through the food production companies while the supply chain was vulnerable. Chomp, chomp. They were more than happy to swallow her company and buy out her contract and ply her with stock options.

Money aside, perhaps the only time to suggest a break in a marriage was after three solid years of togetherness. A real test, that. He wept, of course, as they went over the plans and signed papers and drew up legal documents, the handy template accompanying the brochure. They Zoomed with their lawyer. Reps from the company, PastPresentPerfect, sent long emails and DocuSign documents.

Then she took a car from her home in Vancouver, Washington to Portland for medical exams, all involving instant virus testing, masks, gowns, and gloves. The automated nurse took her blood, while live nurses talked to her from another room. The doctor videoed in while all her systems were observed and scrutinized. Somehow, the pandemic had left Glory lean and strong—all those dog walks and video workouts—and with a heart that literally didn't miss a beat.

Later, she called her children, her friends, everyone inured or stunned into silence. She did get accidentally included in a text thread.

Is she crazy? Dementia like grandma? This is insane!!!!

One laughing-its-ass-off emoji. Then a question mark. Next, ask Dad.

One daughter went the hormone route. Post-meno psychosis?

They were all so bitchy.

Glory's almost off-grid son, the one who blamed the government for the virus and the inability to cure it, only wrote: This isn't a joke.

"Should we get divorced?" Mark asked.

Should they? It wasn't fair to hold him hostage. Besides, being married to a partial corpse wouldn't make him the most eligible bachelor in town. If he were lucky enough to overcome that hurdle, the next woman might want to get married during one of those strange virus lulls, events safe for half a minute.

Of all the people who might be alive in fifty years, Mark was not one of them, unless some other technology emerged while Glory was sleeping. He was alive now, though, and deserved to find the happiness he needed. At this point, Glory had nothing to give him. Sometimes, just before she fell asleep, Mark breathing quietly next to her, she felt the forty or so years of her life left after statis radiate like a sunbeam.

She called her lawyer for a referral. Mark hired a divorce attorney he found on Yelp.

Glory's mother Joan had drifted into dementia. During her last week, Glory went to the visiting platform at Joan's assisted living facility. There her mother sat behind the plexiglass, slumped in a wheelchair, her hand in her caregiver's. Julie had saved Glory's life a hundred times or more. Instead of Glory, Julie was the one there when her mother slipped or cried or worried where California went.

"Do you see it? Am I home yet?" Joan would ask the few times Glory had been able to see her before that third, brutal variant that killed half the remaining folks in the home. "Am I back in Walnut Creek?"

"You are," Glory said. "Isn't it beautiful? Isn't it the most wonderful place in the entire world?"

Whenever Joan asked, Glory and Julie would nod and exclaim over the bright California afternoon, even though the clouds clung to the Cascades. Now Julie would nod her mother to the end. When she turned to leave, Glory waved, cried, finally, remembering her mother when she was young and before life had ruined her. Before Glory's father died and her sister, too. Before her mother started to lose everything, including her mind.

Goodbye, Glory said to all. For now. Maybe forever.

"How is your sleep?"

"I don't sleep much," Glory said. "I haven't probably since menopause. Or I fall asleep immediately, and then I wake up around 1:00 a.m., and then, it's a few hours of horror show dreams, one which involves putting myself into cryogenic sleep for fifty years."

"In the past two weeks, how often have you felt down, depressed, or hopeless?"

"Two weeks? That's all you want to know? What about three years? What about wondering what the point is of any of it? What about wondering if when I wake up in fifty years, I'll want you to put me back under or just kill me because it will still feel pointless?"

"Have you had any thoughts of suicide?"

"Every single day."

"How could you leave your kids?"

"I can't bear to see them suffer, which they will. Eventually. Life is never going to be normal again."

"Do you prefer to stay at home rather than going out and doing new things?"

"Are we supposed to go out and do new things? Really? Where have you been? Don't you watch the charts? Of course, I would rather stay at home. If you could put me under there, that's where I would like to be. At home and totally asleep."

"How is your energy?"

"Gone. For years. I don't have any at all."

This is not how that conversation went.

"Pretty good. Most nights, seven or eight hours."

"I think I've gotten used to the lockdowns. The pattern of them. We know what to expect."

"I don't want to kill myself. That's not what this is about."

"My children are adults. I've talked to them about the entire procedure."

"When we can go out and do safe things, we do. It always makes us feel better."

"I bought an exercise bike, and we walk every morning. I've stayed in shape."

Glory had gone under before, twice for surgeries she awoke from with few side-effects, at least after the waking up part. After her bunionectomy, she'd clawed her way through the cave of anesthesia and found herself weeping.

"Are you crying from pain or emotion?" a nurse asked, her face close to Glory's.

"Emotion," Glory said because she felt nothing, at least in terms of pain. What she felt was that she had been full into perfection and now she was back, here, ripped away from somewhere preferable.

The second time, she did feel pain, or at least she felt her entire body, heavy, uncomfortable, bloated. She'd had a hysterectomy, her uterus pulled through her vagina like a magic trick. Whoosh, the surgeon waving her scrap of flesh like a handkerchief he'd pulled from his hat.

What if, she wondered, delirious, the stiches broke and she opened up, her inner body available to the universe? But she did not seem to be mourning the place she'd been to during her first surgery, that dark hole of peace.

Glory had no idea what she would feel like while asleep for years and years. She had no idea if she would wake up. She worried she would dream for fifty years, a series of relentless nightmares.

She worried when she woke up, she wouldn't remember who she was. Maybe she would wake up fresh, whole, completely blank, a 60-year-old tabula rasa.

Maybe there was no place of peace. All she'd felt was the medication knocking her out. It would be a lot cheaper to succumb to drug addiction, she figured. Alcoholism. She could buy a hookah and quarantine in her family room with bowls of ice cream and popcorn. Her kids might enjoy those visits.

"Are you sure?" Mark whispered one night when they were in bed, the house still and closed down around them.

"No," she said. "I'm not."

The self-driving car dropped her off in front of the building in downtown Portland on a spring Sunday afternoon. There was not one car in the parking lot, and the building in front of her was windowless, grey, absorbing rather than reflecting light. The sky was bright blue like the inside of a buffed sapphire. The wind was mild, the sun angled low in the sky. Above her, Canada geese and the swirl and squeal of swallows.

Glory didn't want additional hard goodbyes. Her family that could be there—her elder daughter and husband had driven for days from Chattanooga—had sat stunned on the family room couch, a stack of legal documents and medical releases in front of them. In a box in the corner, letters to each child for every year. Or, really, Glory had started out that way. By the time she'd gotten into the fourth decade of her long sleep, she'd switched to every five years. The last notes only read, *Hope to see you soon. I love you.*

"Mom?" her daughter had asked, looking up, suddenly alert.

"It's going to be fine," Glory had said.

Her eyes half-closed, Glory kissed them both and then left, empty handed, the car prepaid. If she could have shown up in a hospital gown, she would have. Why bring anything? She didn't need her purse or wallet or keys. No sweater, shoes, coat. No phone or lipstick or breath mints.

They'd told her to not watch movies about cryogenic sleep.

"It's just not like any of that," the technician said as she went over the process in vague terms: slowing of bodily functions, body cooling, energy conservation.

Then bigger words and physics Glory let flow over her like rainwater: vitrification, anti-freezing agent, molecular similarity to glass.

"All of this sounds complicated, but it's nothing Hollywood has gotten right."

"What do you mean?" Glory asked.

The technician rolled her eyes. She was young, and pretty, though Glory wasn't able to see her whole face due to the mask, shield, plexiglass, and six feet of white tile between them. Then, of course, there was the large robotic arm taking samples from Glory's arm, swabbing her nose, throat, and, yes, other parts.

"The pods. The fluid filling up from the bottom and seeming to drown you. So dramatic."

"There is fluid," Glory began. She'd read all the handouts and PDFs and digi-screens.

The technician waved a gloved white hand. Her white bodysuit crinkled noisily. "Of course. But just don't watch."

Glory didn't watch. Or read. Not one movie about space travel billions of light years away or one science fiction novel about climate change and human storage. The technician's words lingered, though, and now, she forced herself to look forward, her eyes on the I-5, the few cars in front of her. There, a bridge. There, a building. Then, she was standing in an empty parking lot, the car purring away. Where had all the people gone? Over the course of the pandemic, three million Americans had died. But that didn't account for this vast emptiness, stillness where once there was laughter and horns and trains rattling their tracks. Once close to here, she and Mark had been stuck for twenty-five minutes as a train inched by pulling cargo containers. Cargo. That was a thing of the past.

Glory turned to face the door that opened for her, a swooshing maw that sucked her right in and closed with a hissing whisper. Wrapping her arms around herself, Glory walked forward.

"Glory?"

Something parted, a hand reaching through a black curtain and then pulling back.

"Glory?"

This time, she felt her face, though she was still surrounded by darkness.

"Glory?"

Her eyes twitched, and she allowed herself to look through the slits of light that seemed far away, tiny windows she had to squint to see through.

"Glory. Glory. There you are. You're awake," the voice said, a man's sing-songy voice.

She imagined she was nodding. She wasn't sure she could feel her body, though she began to feel her heft, her bones, weight, substance. Gravity overcame her. Her spine was flat on a surface. Her toes were bare.

"Glory," the voice said after what seemed like years.

And there, she felt her lungs filling up with air. Then she exhaled, her throat scratchy, sore, lungs flat like science exhibits. Pain or emotion? Pain.

Glory opened her eyes.

It took nearly three months for Glory to be able to stay awake longer than an hour without nodding off no matter what position or place she was in. This utter somnolence certainly hadn't been in the brochure, but the good news was that PastPresentPerfect didn't kick her out on her rear—that rehab clause that convinced her to sign up in the first place must be in full effect. They were bound to get her to the state she'd been in when she'd walked through the door. Sentient, standing, sound.

But Glory wasn't close to that door or in that building or even in Portland, much less the United States. Most people around her were speaking French, a language she failed to pass three times by her reckoning: high school, college, adult ed. Sometimes, she thought she heard English in the hallways. Or maybe it was Dutch or German. Finally, she was able to get up, eat, shower (if you could call the contraption a shower), dress, and find a chair in the bright white solarium.

"When will my relatives come?" she had asked from the time she could speak again.

The technicians wagged fingers and tskked. She'd been told, more than once. When her body was ready, so would her mind be. Then they would reveal everything.

They dressed her in soft, rumpled clothing, all in light colors, white, gray, fawn. They gave her a mirror when she asked, and yes, she reminded herself of herself, so she handed it back, not wanting to do any further analysis, not yet.

Glory read children's stories set in England that featured hedgerows, unicorns, and vast swaths of lawn. And like a child, she ate very bland food—porridge or pudding? Soup or smoothie? First using a walker-type contraption that seemed to float around her, Glory let an attendant lead her round and round the building, which was round, the ceilings opaque glass that let in only a filtered silver light.

The air smelled clean and fresh, massaged by air filters, lightened by the essence of citrus and lavender.

Warm water baths, massage, and sleep. More bland food. Sleep. Then, finally, a short talk with the woman who seemed to be in change. Glory blinked when she walked toward her table in the common room. The woman's hair was a cumulus above her, dark and ecstatic.

"You're doing quite well," the woman said. She said her name was Zi, her voice was filled with a place far away from the Pacific Northwest.

Glory looked at Zi and shrugged. What were the comparisons? she wondered. How many of her kind were staggering around like Frankenstein's monster?

"How can you tell?" Glory asked.

Zi stared straight at her as if to say, *Look around you.*

The room—really, everywhere—was sparsely populated. One person at a table there, another walking past here. She'd only gotten to nodding acquaintance with one or two others. No one seemed to want to talk. Maybe curiosity was one of the last things to return to the recently thawed brain.

Glory put her hands flat on the table.

Zi waved open something in the space between them, a screen

they could both read that appeared magically out of nothing in 3D.

Glory Matthews. 4/15/2026. The date Glory walked through the door.

"What went wrong?" Glory said after a long silence.

Zi opened up another screen with a whisk of her hand. It all played out in front of Glory like one of those documentaries she and Mark used to watch on the History Channel. But this had no voiceovers or captions, images only. There, the people in line for vaccines. There, people in their hospital beds. More and more and more, enough so that Glory shot Zi a look. Zi nodded, indicated that Glory should keep watching, which she did, finally seeing the world lug its way out of illness, war, famine, despair, and chaos. Then new cities, solar and wind-powered everything, populations looking relieved, but wary, stunned but living.

Fifty years had been a low-ball estimate. PastPresentPerfect hadn't nailed down the perfect part.

"Well," Glory said. "Things did not go as planned."

Zi looked down at her hands. "They did not."

"You kept me alive," Glory said.

"You paid for that—"

"I know—"

Zi held up a hand, her smooth face serious. "Your contract stipulated that if necessary, we could perform emergency medical procedures during your sleep."

"Like my what? Appendix was going to burst, right?"

Zi gave her the serious look again, and something (not her appendix) inside Glory twisted.

"We had hundreds of thousands of clients in deep sleep, and we were able to use their—"

"My?"

"Your tissues were used to help several large-scale, world-wide companies create a database to facilitate testing procedures that eventually led to a final cure for the virus. The latest and last variant. The pandemic is finally over."

Glory sat back. She'd never been a scientist, but she was sure she couldn't have been "sampled" while frozen. How, then, to thaw and refreeze bodies? Never worked well on chicken breasts, that was for sure. Freezer burn all around.

"That doesn't seem to be my personal medical emergency, though," Glory said.

"It was a world emergency," Zi said, tapping closed the screen between them. "You ended up saving yourself."

Glory knew her mouth was hanging open and shut it too quickly, rattling a tooth. Zi gave her a what-can-I-say expression, hands up. "You signed your consent."

"I suppose," Glary said. Point was, though, she wasn't missing her tissues at this point. She watched Zi, waiting for more.

"You were awakened three times in the past ninety years," Zi said finally. "This is your fourth awakening, and your last."

Glory looked at her hands. She was still sixty years old. "How long then?"

"One hundred and twenty-five years," Zi said.

Lord. Glory thought of something she'd heard long ago (really long ago now). *In a hundred years, all new people.* So true. That's all it took. She was in the land of all new people. Her mother, husband (ex), and children gone.

Glory breathed in deeply once, twice. She swallowed. "Why don't I remember any of the other times you woke me up?"

"We kept you in an unconscious state," Zi said.

"But I'm awake now," Glory said, wanting to make sure.

"You are."

Zi explained that Glory was in a facility near Paris, one she and some of the sleeping were relocated to during the first North

American war. The EU had formed a scientific amnesty program that kept PastPresentPerfect clients alive and safe, at least as much as possible.

"Why would they do that?" Glory blurted.

Zi held up a hand and went on. Twenty-five percent of the clients perished during a defrosting (Glory now thought of popsicles and ice cream and frozen corn). Some were permanently altered by the process and were euthanized (legal now) by family consent (another part of the contract Glory neglected to read, fucking lawyer). And now, there was a slow process of revitalizing and awakening the remaining clients, giving them time to acclimate (if that were possible) and releasing them to their families, should there be anyone left. In any case, they were being given hero benefits for saving humanity. A place to live and a pension paid by various countries.

Glory turned to look out the window, though there was nothing to see but light. She hoped she didn't have to hear what had happened to her family, sorrow surely in the narratives. *First* North American War? How many had there been? She'd save that gumball for later.

The days stretched on, Glory reading about the past few decades but mostly enjoying being outside in the atrium breathing in fresh air when they opened the retractable roof. They gave her work boots and a trowel and a plot of warm earth. Something she had been holding tight to her ribs and spine and pelvis relaxed, opened, and she hunkered down near the squash plants, digging up weeds.

She and Mark had had a garden in the first house they lived in, rows of basil and tomatoes, the end of summer awash in balsamic vinegar, olive oil, salt, and pepper.

When her children were little, Glory had taught them how to plant, all of them staring down into the two-inch holes they'd made with trowels just like these. They'd been so bright, little lights burning steady next to her.

If she stilled and closed her eyes, she could imagine them all at the dining table. All those voices, hands, Mark looking at her, eyebrows raised. They'd been in that family together, at least for a while. Shoulders touching as they pushed their family wheel forward.

How had Glory given up on that momentum? Them? She wiped her nose with the back of a white sleeve and blinked back into her tasks. Aerate, amend, attend. Over and over again.

"We have a surprise for you," Zi said. "Yours is a very unusual case."

Turning from the window, Glory rested her gaze on Zi. What a job. Telling the unfrozen what awaited them.

"Do tell." Glory smiled to lighten her sarcasm. Her worst habit.

Zi smiled for the first time since Glory had met her. "Your husband. We woke him up two months ago. Soon, he'll be ready to see you."

Glory blinked. Had they married her to another client while partially thawed? Were she and another melted popsicle now together for eternity?

"What do you mean?"

Zi blinked and, for the first time since sitting down, seem confused. "Your husband, Mark."

"My husband didn't do this with me. He stayed at home. He was going to get remarried and live on without me."

Zi scrolled through the screen, finding another date and name to illuminate. Mark Matthews 7/22/2026.

"That's very odd," Glory said. "Why would he follow me?"

"Why indeed," Zi said.

Mark smiled at her the way he used to pre-virus. Maybe even the way he had before they'd had jobs and kids, mortgages and cars and bills. He seemed rumpled, beaten down, and maybe not all there yet. But happy, like a toddler who knew that soon it would be lunch and then nap time and then play.

"It will take you both some time to settle into yourselves," Zi said while the attendants walked Mark into the common room to sit with Glory near the window's glow.

The attendants backed away, leaving them to stare at each other.

"I don't get it," Glory said. "You never liked this plan."

Mark's smile faded a bit but not by much. "It started to make sense. Of course, I never could have known. . ."

He lifted a hand, the same hand she had seen what felt like only months before. But 125 years had passed. She reached over and grabbed it, and for the first time since she woke up, Glory began to cry. Soon, she was on his lap, both of them in tears, clutching each other. Both of them survivors of war and pestilence. Both of them *les survivants*, as people called them.

"What are we going to do?" Glory asked finally.

"Live?" Mark wiped his face. "Go on?"

"Why not?"

Maybe, Glory thought, she was ready to try that now.

Turned out, they had relatives, three great-grandsons and their families who lived in what was now the country carved out of parts of Washington, Oregon, and California. Alliance Federation. What a mouthful.

Glory and Mark had chatted with them via some kind of futuristic 3D app, the Zoom of the way-in-the-future times.

Their two older children's children had survived the viruses and the wars, and these great-grandsons had been put in charge of their frozen great-grandparents.

"We're lucky," one of them said, Davi, a handsome man in his mid-sixties. They could all be friends and go on a cruise together (if such things still existed), Glory thought. Pals heading into old age. "We made it through."

Glory wasn't ready to hear about her own children's fate, not yet. So she asked questions about her great-grandchildren, the scientist, engineer, farmer. All of them had Mark's dark eyes.

"We'll come visit," Davi and the others said, waving as the call ended.

"Imagine that," Mark said when their images flickered away.

She barely could.

Of course, she still hated things about her husband. He didn't ask enough questions about her or really care what she was doing with the cheeses in the cheese cave. He didn't know the names of the cow and goats and was woefully ignorant about the drainage at the south side of their property. He wouldn't gather eggs or pull weeds in the vegetable garden. Worst of all, he was excelling in French, mingling better with their neighbors and able to go to the local *taverne* to drink with his new fellows.

But he knew how to work the ancient (relatively) massive oven in the wide-open kitchen and made the most amazing coq au vin with the *coq* that wasn't chicken at all, but a protein invented during some lean economic times. Now, eating animals was forbidden. They could be milked or sustainably shorn or petted. They could sleep in your bed, run roughshod through the garden, or be brought into public spaces. You could (with a permit) use their milk to make cheese but not their flesh to make *pâté*. No meatloaf. No sausage.

"Score one for the beasts of the field!" Mark said when discovering this nice twist, he a long-time vegetarian.

"Not to mention the birds of the air."

When Glory potted plants and fed the chickens, cats wound around her ankles. The dogs barked at the ravens. Day and night and day again. Fall came, the leaves a crackling red. Late, the world dark, she and Mark curled together on the couch, wondering what they would wake up from next.

The Brightness of Things

"Maxine Whitshaw?" the man on the phone said after Max's hello.

"Yes?" Max clenched her cell phone between her collarbone and the tip of her chin. At that moment, she was on a stepstool, looking for her father's baton. The back of the cupboard over the fridge was a place no one ever put anything, so she'd waited to search here till nothing else offered up the stick. Of course, there it had been, hiding at the back.

"My name is Davis Smith. From Precise Aeronautics."

Her phone in one hand, the baton in the other, she backed off the stool, staring at the stainless steel door of the enormous fridge her husband Ronnie had insisted on during the remodel. With three children under ten, thirty fingers between them, the front was a collage of smudgy handprints with milk, peanut butter, and strawberry jam embellishments.

Davis Smith waited on the line. Max tried to think why anyone from any aeronautic company would call her.

"Huh?" She put the baton on the granite counter top and pulled the phone away from her face, looking at the number. A strange area code. Richmond, Virginia.

"You entered the lottery—"

Max shook her head, snorted. Phone spam. Telemarketers. Desperate people making money desperately. She hung up and slid the phone into her dress pocket. Picking up the baton, she twirled it a bit, remembering her father using it with much more gravitas. In front of an orchestra, raising it in his hand, the room silent. And then down with a flourish. *Waaah*—the sounds of every instrument filling the air. Her mother sitting still next to her, rapt as they both stared at Max's father's sleek black hair.

Max's phone buzzed, and she pressed the button to silence it. After she gave her eldest child, Hazel, the baton (a potential prop for the school spring play), she'd get online and re-up her number for the no-call list.

But later, sitting at the computer, her phone buzzed again. And again, it was Davis Smith.

"Don't hang up. I'm serious."

"About what?" Max asked.

"About the lottery. No one believes me the first time. Mostly, it takes me four calls. I've resorted to texts."

Max paused, clicked on the no-call list's "submit." The form zinged into the ether, she sat back in her chair and waited for Davis to finish. After she got rid of him, she was free and clear for what? Three years? She must have not re-upped when she was supposed to.

"Candygram," she said. "Might work."

"Candygram?" Davis asked. She imagined him writing down the suggestion.

"Stripper," Max went on, sitting back in her computer chair. "Stripper singing telegram. Vienna Boys Choir. Something big, Davis."

"This is big, Maxine."

At the bottom of her computer, her email notification popped up. A message from Precise Aeronautics. Lottery winner, it read. Space Shuttle.

"Who are you?" Max asked, leaning toward her computer, her elbows resting on the wood. Pages she should have been editing crinkled under her forearms.

Precise.

"I told you. I'm calling from Precise Aeronautics." Davis was weary. "I'm calling to let you know you won the trip."

"The trip."

"To the moon."

"I won a trip to the moon," Max said flatly, but something flashed in her memory. Something on a website. A travel site. In order to join, she had to enter to win. She must have. All she'd really wanted to do was look at the photos of Portugal and Tanzania. The ocean. A safari. Anything but read other people's bad writing. So she'd given out her email and her phone number. And voilà! Davis called. Not that Precise would really send her. How could they? There would be regulations and things that she would fail. Probably the weight requirement (of course, perhaps one weighed less on the moon. Or was it more? In space, she'd be light as air). But here? On an Earth scale? She'd be done. Over. A goner. Total failure, as with so many endeavors. Just last night. That tomato sauce. And the baton? Hazel had wanted it this morning. Hadn't Max needed to rush it to the school about fifteen minutes ago? Wasn't the audition going on right now without a proper conductor's baton?

"Look, I know this seems crazy. But our founder wants to make Precise Aeronautics' moon missions accessible. For the people."

"Mostly rich people," Max said. She knew about Rupert Forsythe. Wacky, wild, crazy British loopster who already owned everything and was now expanding his empire off-world. His dyed blond wig-like mop. His crazy black eyebrows. A hip Groucho Marx.

"We are scheduling our first four flights. We estimate the first in five months. August 15th, to be precise. You will be on our third voyage."

"I won," Max said.

"I'll say," Davis said. Max could almost hear him wipe his brow.

"Just think. One-point-four million people filled out the entry form. And you? One of four winners! Maxine, it's a miracle."

It turned out that not being on the first voyage was the miracle. Crash landing, no survivors. Not even that flight's lottery winner. Forsythe went back to the drawing board.

"We will have to postpone your take-off," Davis told her on one of his monthly calls. She'd filled out all the forms (liability, for one, clearly necessary), gone to the doctor (her weight was just fine), completed all the blood work and scans, taken the shots, and started a diet and exercise regime. In the coming months, she would head off to space camp to learn about anti-gravity and dehydrated food. All that was left was to tell her family.

"Not surprising." Max sat at her desk, the computer screen open to a memoir about growing up in a cage. When she received the manuscript, Max wondered if she'd endure the reading, the author's life a harrowing experience of survival. But the prose ached for verbs and detail. Confined, trapped, tortured, stuck were strangely absent from the long narrative.

"You aren't a writer," the managing editor told her once. "You're a copy editor. So stop suggesting stuff you shouldn't. Your bailiwick? Commas. Semicolons. Anachronisms. Number format. Come on, Max!"

"It's all been figured out," Davis told her. "Really. It had something to do with batteries. Simple."

"How many people died?"

Davis was silent for a moment. "I know. But you don't have to worry. Your family doesn't have to worry."

Max imagined that her husband Ronnie would not be worried. At all. In fact, he'd probably pack her moon case.

"Just let me know if it's going to be real," Max said. "You know, people do have lives. Going to the moon takes some time out of the schedule. People have responsibilities."

"Do they?" Davis said, his voice heavy with too many phone calls.

"You're right. Probably not. But let me know, okay?"

"Will do." Davis hung up.

"Who was that?" Hazel asked. Max turned towards her office door. Her daughter stood there clutching her school backpack. She looked exactly as Max had as a child, except pretty. Dark hair, dark eyes, slight and small. But there was a sweet softness about the eyes and lips. That was Ronnie. And the boys were him exactly, no evidence of Max in their long bones, bright faces, thick, dark blond hair. Even though John and Ryan were only five and seven, everyone always noted they'd be "lady killers."

What a thing to say.

Max formed her lie. "A man who has a job for me. But it keeps not happening."

Hazel nodded. She understood about the vagaries of editing. The influx of work and then the spaces of nothing in Max's life. Ronnie, on the other hand, was a constant working machine. Up at 5:30 am, home at 7:00 pm. Golf (or so he said) on one or two weekend afternoons.

"Clients," he had said when she first complained about having to drive the children to every activity and party and soccer match by herself. "You know the game."

Max did know the game, and she hadn't been thinking about investment banking.

"When will the job happen?" Hazel asked as they walked down the hall toward the kitchen. John and Ryan still had another hour to sleep before Max had to wake them up. At nine years old, Hazel took the early bus, finally free from her brothers' questions and demands.

"In a blue moon," Max wanted to say but didn't. "When the cows jump."

She didn't say that either.

"Soon, I hope," Max said. "But don't worry. I'll tell you when it happens."

When Hazel sat at the table, she turned to rummage through her backpack. "Here," she said, holding out the baton. Max had made it to the final performance, the baton becoming Hazel's witch wand.

Max took it, the wood smooth under her hand. She could almost feel the old music.

"I've arranged everything," Max said, her duffel bag packed and by the front door.

"You're shitting me, right?" Ronnie stood in front of the fireplace. "You think you're going to the moon?"

"I am going to the moon," Max said.

"What about the kids?"

"I told them already. Precise has a live feed they can watch from the computer. There's a kind of Skype thing. I showed Hazel—"

"Shit!" Ronnie stomped around, pushing one hand through his blond but greying hair. When they'd met in college, it had shone white. He'd been a Nordic dream-god-man to Max's flirty, gamin, fake self-image. For a while, it had worked.

"They crashed the first time!" Ronnie shouted. "What am I supposed to do if that happens?"

"Shhh." Max stood, glossing over the whole topic. "Stop it. Yes, they crashed. But not the second time. Things went perfectly."

"Did you see them up there?" Ronnie waved his hands skyward. "In that moon house. What is that guy thinking? British nutjob, that's what he is. God. Yes, that's it! He thinks he's God!"

Max picked up her duffel bag. The children were in bed. Betsy, the nanny, was coming at six the next morning, just before Ronnie left for work. Max had showed the children her photo online, a middle-aged woman with short gray hair and kind brown eyes.

In preparation, Max had posted a detailed schedule for the two weeks she'd be gone: school, classes, and parties. There were meals stacked like flat shiny astronauts in the freezer. Lasagna, mac and cheese, meatballs, vegetable soup. Betsy would have Max's car and sleep in the guest room. Precise was picking up the cost.

"You're really going to the moon, Mommy?" John had asked, his blue eyes wide as the Earth she would soon be looking down upon. Innocent, for now.

"I am, sweetie."

"Can I come?"

By the time John was an adult, people like Forsythe would be running daily shuttles to the moon and the moon spas. Maybe even Mars. After all, NASA had just made it to Pluto. In a few years, Ronnie could golf on the scorched, oxygen-empty ground under a bubble. Maybe his game would improve.

Max put her hand on the doorknob. Outside, a Lyft driver waited. "Look, you know you're only upset that the schedule is rattled. Bottom line, it's a relief. A break. Right?"

Ronnie stilled, watched her, his wide eyes John's.

"I'll be back in two weeks. A little less," Max said, opening the door and stepping out onto the porch, the moonlight—no, it was streetlight—all around her.

Since all the space shuttle incidents and NASA's folding up of manned inter-moon and planetary missions, Max hadn't bothered to keep up with the latest developments. Actually, she never really had. But she'd watched the news, seen the rockets go up and the shuttles hurtle down. She'd seen them blow up a couple of times, shards and chunks tumbling towards the earth, black and smoking. The spectators pressing hands against agonized mouths, disbelief and then horror in their eyes.

But now things had changed. The shuttle was like a small powerful jet, beefy and thick, nose and body like a squat but powerful porpoise.

"Can it actually lift off?" a man next to her asked. He'd been on the chartered plane she'd boarded at LAX. Now they were in the California desert, the exact location a secret.

"Enough so that it can crash," another man answered. "Jack."

He held out his hand first to the other man (Mario) and then to Max.

They were sitting in a waiting area, bags at their feet, looking out a window at a group of six other people walking down the tarmac past the shining, stubby shuttle towards the building in which they all sat. Max realized she was only one of two women. Two among seven. Something pinged in her. An alert. A siren. A siren.

Max introduced herself, her heart beating in her throat. She was going to the moon. With these people. Strangers. It was like the first day of school.

The door whooshed open, pulling in hot air. From another door, the instructor who had greeted Max initially and two other similarly-garbed people (one a woman) came in, carrying bags and clipboards. The room filled with noise, the stilted loudness of the first hour of an awkward cocktail party.

The woman walked around handing out the bags, which were actually backpacks, and one of the men passed out the clipboards. The first man—Marshall—stood at the front of the room and called for everyone's attention.

"Thank you all for getting here on schedule. I know how hard that can be with other airlines," Marshall said, giving the group a wink. There were polite laughs. "But this won't be like any other airline that you've been on. After some training, you will be going to a place no one else flies to. Can't fly to. And no one but Precise has a groundbreaking, state-of-the-art moon unit."

Marshall looked around the room, wide-eyed and waiting, but whatever he was waiting for didn't happen.

"He must have named it 'moon unit,'" Jack whispered into Max's ear. "Wants a pat on the back."

Max turned a little to take in Jack. He smelled clean and rich, all the fibers on his body brand-spanking new. His underwear was probably never worn and the highest quality. He probably didn't even buy it himself, Max thought. His wife. His butler. His maid. His housekeeper. Or, at least, Amazon. His hair was a rich dark brown, a cap on his perfectly featured head. He was what? Thirty? A specimen from the permanently rich, a lucky fellow whose college degree was just trimming.

She was only thirty-five, permanently middle-class, and mostly educated, but she knew where the name of their moon abode came from. She just didn't have the energy to explain that the musician Frank Zappa named his daughter exactly that: Moon Unit.

Jack smiled when he noticed her gaze. His skin was like lightly browned butter. Obviously, he was not one of the lottery winners. No, Jack, with his new clothes, shiny leather shoes, and perfect skin paid 1.2 million for his moon vacation.

"For these first few days, however," Marshall continued, "you will be training on our space shuttle, The Vivant."

Marshall turned towards the window, motioning with one sweeping arm at the shuttle they'd all been staring at anyway.

Everyone clapped, as if forgetting, Max thought, the nine people who died on the other shuttle. What was it called? As she clapped, she racked her brain. Oh, yeah. The Gift.

That keeps giving.

"So please follow Charlotte into the barracks. It's unisex. Just like everything. Bathrooms included. The future is here at Precise."

Max clomped behind the crowd, her backpack swinging on her arm. She looked at the clipboard and the list of names as they walked out of the building and across the tarmac: Jack, Anne, Steve, Thom, Mario, Bruce, Jorge, Xavier, Maxine. Just like in school. Off to learn something but at the back, the end, as usual.

Except, she was very good at moving around in the anti-gravity simulator, a large Quonset hut of joy on the edge of the training facility. She'd been a good swimmer and had even been on the diving team one year. Her back still arched. Her feet flexed. Bouncing was her specialty. But in her space suit and alone in air, every muscle moved in concert.

"You're a mermaid!" Anne said.

Maxine turned round and round, one knee bent, pushing herself as she indeed had under water.

"Quite a spinner," Jack said as he sailed by. Jorge gave her a dark glance as she spun away from her own air circle. He was "Whore-Hey." At least, that's how she remembered to say his name. He zipped past her. Even without gravity, she could smell his aftershave, the kind that only a CIA operative could wear. Amber and ice.

Steve, Thom, Mario, and Xavier looked like arctic boy scouts in their white belted suits, all of them clumped together at one end of the simulator. They grabbed at each other, spun around, laughing, flinging each other in ever-widening arcs. It was hard to believe they were, in order, a state senator, a social media company mega-millionaire, a tennis champion, and a movie star-slash-icon.

Only Bruce—corporate lawyer—seemed allergic to weightlessness, thundering and bumping around the tube like a broken bumblebee. "Uh," he moaned. "Uh."

The rest of them? A *corps de ballet*.

They slept for three nights in the barracks. They were heavy in their beds, back on Earth for another twelve hours. Anne spun under her stiff blankets, the sound a crackling ratchet amongst the male complement of snores. A best-selling advice columnist, Anne was more used to the Ritz and Four Seasons than boot camp bed rolls.

"I just want to get the hell out of here," she whispered. The barracks may have been co-ed, but Max and Anne had segregated themselves at the far wall.

"Aren't you scared we'll crash?" Max asked. This after a panicked Skype with Ronnie and the children. She hadn't shown it, answering their questions, showing off her fancy suit. But after the call ended, the shaking started, every system—those very ones she learned about in high school physiology—heaved in her body as if trying to escape. How dare she try to take them off planet!

"There are worse ways," Anne said. And she would know. All those emails. All those letters. All that pain. "Anyway, the last one made it."

"Two days is a long time on the moon," Max whispered.

"It's a long time anywhere," Anne said.

"What are we going to do there?" Max asked. "Play cards? Charades? Write? Watch Netflix?"

Anne was silent, and for a second, Max thought she was crying. The terror had finally caught up with her, all her advice run out, even for herself. But the herky-jerky sound under the terrible blankets wasn't crying. It was laughter, the sound Max finally fell asleep to.

After the fear that they would die on liftoff passed, the shuttle takeoff seemed almost normal. If she hadn't been looking out the window, Max might have thought she was on the United Airlines Flight 930 to London, a red-eye, only 36,000 feet above the earth, speeding over Greenland. The Vivant, under her seated body, whirred and chugged, the noise deafening even with earplugs and a helmet. She felt the G-forces press her against the seat, but the pressure was like a large hand, constantly but patiently subduing her. A constant takeoff, a flight manned by a novice pilot, hard and jerky but not death-defying.

And she was looking out the window, her face pressed against the quadruple-paned but tiny glass porthole. She was hurtling up past that whisk of white, oxygen, the atmosphere, the earth below a swirling orb of blue and enormous cloud, just like in the posters.

You are here. A red arrow pointed to the planet.

But she wasn't there. Not anymore. Not after the flare of sparks and heat as they passed through the thing that made them earthlings, the technology Forsythe paid billions for. *Pop!*, and they were space creatures. *Pop!*, and Max was untethered. Free.

As per the lecture at space camp, there was a surge. A rocket firing from the back of the shuttle, and then they were propelled towards the moon, fueled by an ion drive, whatever that really was. For the next three days—Marshall had outlined the trajectory on the PowerPoint—they would complete the 384-kilometre journey, achieve lunar orbit, and then land, a process that involved a portion of the shuttle detaching like an escape pod from any number of sci-fi movies. From the pod landing site, they would be picked up by the moon shuttle and taken to the Moon Unit, where they would stay for two nights, though Max questioned the notion of night on the moon. Dark side, bright side? Where would they be in relation to the sun? Or the earth, for that matter? Obviously, she hadn't been paying much attention. She decided to not worry about it because at this point, strung up in the deep dark space speckled with pinpricks of light and stars, there was very little she could do about anything.

Also, as soon as the seat belt sign was turned off (yes, really) and the cabin attendant went to check on the pilot and crew, Max understood what Anne's plan for the next few days entailed.

The rustling sounds came from Anne's sleeping cubicle. Then that laughter. Clearly, she and Xavier (missing from the cabin) had taken off their helmets and suits, using the convenient openings in their compression skin suits to free important body parts for the activity at hand.

"What kind of club is this? The ten-thousand-mile-high club?" Bruce asked as he bumped by, floating, sort of, as he grabbed from chair back to chair back. He wasn't that heavy, Max thought. But he was resisting buoyancy, urging himself to ground even when there wasn't any ground.

Max almost asked him what he meant, but then remembered sex in airplane bathrooms occurring at a high cruising altitude. She and Ronnie had never had sex on an airplane, not even a grounded one. Or really any place other than a bed, usually their bed. Hazel had already been on board when they got married, so they had rarely travelled together, save for those few months before Hazel's birth. But from the moment of her daughter's conception, Max had been queasy and wan, preferring to stay home rather than accompany Ronnie on his regular trips to New York and London, places they'd enjoyed. Before marriage. Before children. Before they stopped wanting to be together.

Anne's low, guttural laugh had no gravity, filling the shuttle from floor to ceiling, though, of course, it was hard to know which was which at this point.

Bucket list, Max thought. Have sex in space.

Bucket list. Have sex on the moon.

Max floated to the observation platform, which was a stretch of the term, the space only as big as a normal rear airplane galley, but unlike the rest of the craft it had two larger windows. Jack bobbed in front of one, staring down at the earth, taking photos with his phone. He turned when he noticed Max.

"Fancy a drink?"

Jack wasn't British, so Max questioned the "fancy." Also, she questioned drinking,

though the spacecraft attendant had shown them the self-serve liquor vault as they boarded.

"Isn't one in space like ten on the ground?"

"We're drunk without even having started." Jack flipped the latch and switch for the vault. "Grey Goose?"

Despite the alcohol, it wasn't Jack that was first. One tiny Grey Goose, and Max floated to the back of the shuttle, her eyes shut, the empty bottle clutched in her hand. She woke with Mario next to her, both of them wedged in his sleeping pod. His hands ran up and down her compression suited body, hers on his. And wow! Even covered with tight material, Mario was a star, the tennis victories written all over each muscle. His body radiated like a pulsar, his heartbeat a slow one-two even as he panted in her drunken ear.

As she moaned in pleasure, she wished she were just a bit more conscious. She wanted to remember her infidelity, at least enough to feel super guilty about it later. There was more panting and some groaning, and then nothing but space all around them.

In the hours before entering the moon's orbit, there was Thom. She'd read a lot about him—hard not to when she spent a portion of every day on his company's social media site—and though she'd never really imagined all this pre-moon sex, she would have assumed the billionaire would be the one having it. Because he could.

But he was quiet in bed, pulling Max on top, their suits grinding away together. This time she was sober, and as he closed his eyes, grimacing in pleasure—or what substituted for it—Max watched him, her body going on without her thoughts. She'd gotten past the guilt and shame of infidelity after Mario (things seemed to happen faster in space) so she wondered, as Thom pushed inside her, how he had been the one to make all that money. What choices had he made that she had not? And yet, here they were, together, in space. Sure, she'd won her trip. Sure, she was just a part-time copy editor with three children living in the suburbs. In a failing marriage, or at least a disentangling one. But now? Here? She and Thom Buckingham were even.

They woke to the voice of the pilot, telling them to return to their seats.

"Man," said Thom, his blue-green gaze on hers. How many times had she seen this face? None, really. Only once in real life, here on this trip. Not that this trip was real.

"Yeah," Max said, and they floated out of the pod and clambered into their space suits and helmets, allowing the attendant to assist them. Back in their seats, all of them strapped in and locked down, the orbit and landing protocols began.

Xavier said, "One small step for man…" and then seemed to forget the rest. Next there were thrusters and trajectories. The cabin detached, and they plunged down, stars, space, and Max's whole life flashing past her little window.

What was Hazel doing right now? Was she laughing? Were the boys in their bath? Had they eaten their broccoli at dinner? Was Ronnie coming home at night? Did he read them stories?

Something seemed to yank them up, Max's breath jumping to the roof of her mouth. And then they settled, settled, settled, and clanged down. She opened her eyes, not realizing she'd jammed them shut and tight. Turning toward the window, she saw the white, pocked, pillowy surface of the moon.

"What's all that damn mess out there?" Steve asked, his voice Southern and raspy. She hadn't slept with him, yet. Maybe Anne had. All his fundamentalist preaching might be just be for show.

"Space garbage. Leftover landing junk."

"Maybe you should lobby for a recycling program, Steve," Thom said.

In her headset, Max heard people sniggering. Thom was a notorious environmentalist. At least online. In reality, he had torn down an entire San Francisco block of historical houses and gardens to build his new twelve-thousand-square-foot mansion that he shared with his neurosurgeon wife.

The attendant was up, releasing the seat locks, helping them out of their bindings. There was a clunk at the door. They all walked toward the back, carrying the few belongings they were allowed. In her spacesuit, Max felt like the Pillsbury Doughboy. With her helmet, a goldfish. And yet, she kept hearing HAL's voice saying, "I'm sorry, Dave. I'm afraid I can't do that."

But the moon shuttle's door stayed open, and they all filed in, the attendants closing the doors, leaving the cabin behind at the moon landing site. Then they bounced off, heading to the moon unit. Climate controlled, gravity at almost normal ("You'll feel like you've had a cleanse," Marshall had said. "At least five pounds lighter!"), the Moon Unit would attempt to replicate the atmosphere on earth. They'd be back on ground, using their own bones and muscles to keep upright.

As she peered through the window, Max watched the shuttle bound and surge over the moon, past mounds of more junk, dipping down into a valley where she soon saw a building in the distance. At first, it seemed like an assortment of igloos, but as the shuttle barreled ever forward, she noted that each igloo was interconnected by tubes. As they rounded the first igloo, she saw there was a giant igloo in the center, all tubes leading toward the center. Out the other side of the shuttle, she noted a farm of solar panels, all gleaming silver in the harsh sunlight.

After a few moments, the shuttle slowed and another docking procedure ensued. Air hissed. Parts clanged together. A lurch. A stop. A lurch. A stop. She could almost hear HAL. "Just what do you think you're doing, Dave?"

Then the attendants were up, freeing the passengers from yet another set of restraints. Silently, in a row, they all walked toward the exit. At the rear, Max counted how many people she hadn't slept with.

As if checking into a Four Seasons room with a personal concierge, and once they'd taken off their spacesuits and hung them in a "coat room" near the entrance, they were led individually to their own private igloo. Or piece of an igloo.

"You're going to love it up here," the young man said. He was dressed as though this were a Carnival cruise. Nautical epaulets on his shoulders (gold and black). A white short-sleeved shirt, white pants, soft velvety white shoes. "Forsythe has made the moon accessible."

Some tag line, she thought, almost laughing. But then she realized it likely was the tag line.

After a tour of the accommodations, the young man in white left, the doors whooshing behind him. Max stared out her oval window, blinking into the glare of the moon, darkness hovering over the white. She dug through her bag to find the device Precise had given them, an iPad on steroids.

She clicked, and in what felt like a long time (and how could it not be longer?), Ronnie's face was on her screen. He smiled, the screen wavered, stilled, and then he was back.

"Are you there?"

She nodded, unable to say a word. Instead, she picked up the device and walked it over to the window. Max heard Ronnie call for the kids, and then as she held the screen out toward the moon and the vast black of nothingness all around her, she heard their sounds of awe. What other sounds were possible?

After a minute, she gave them the same tour of her pod that she'd been given. More sounds of awe. But then she had to look at them, all three kids in front, their smiles, two gap-toothed, one not. But all beaming. Ronnie, in the back, smiling at her in a way he hadn't for years. All of them were wide-eyed, open-mouthed as if breathless, staring at her as if she'd done more than just enter a lottery.

She had to hang up, so she did, telling them she had to get to dinner. But what she did instead was lie back on the large but very hard bed and fall asleep.

Everyone was assembled at the large table, including Forsythe himself, who must have stayed on after the last flight. The artificial light that filled the room shone on his full head of over-dyed blond hair that stuck up straight and seemed held to his head like a hat. His teeth were as white as the moon, and as he talked he waved one hand like a dancer. Or a conductor, his movements punctuating every sentence. Every word, even.

Davis was young and lean, tight and trim like the young man who'd shown Max to her room. In fact, all the men seemed that way. When introduced to Max, he beamed, teeth as white as his boss's.

Attendants buzzed around the table, putting down plates filled with food that must have arrived on the latest shuttle. Bowls of vegetables, plates of sliced meats. Potatoes and rice and pasta. Max sat back in her chair, watching them all. Even off earth, they had more than the 99 percent. They were sitting on a rock with no air or water but living like they had them anyway.

The attendants made a show of popping corks, and Bruce whispered in her ear, "One on the moon is like twenty on Earth."

When everyone had been served, Forsythe raised his glass. "To those of you who made—"

Bruce whispered, "Survived."

"—the trip," Forsythe continued, "may this adventure be the first of many and lead to a new colony for humankind."

"Bet you're glad he said human and not man." Bruce bent over his glass, hiding his laughter. Clearly he was headed toward that twenty on Earth.

They all clinked glasses and started eating, Max finally hungry. She'd barely eaten on the shuttle ride, certain at first that she would die and then a little too busy to take much time out for a snack. Now, it was as if she was starving.

"One pound on the moon is twenty on Earth," Bruce hiccupped, pouring himself another glass.

Across the table, Xavier was leaning toward Anne, whispering in her ear. Anne's gaze bore into Max, so she turned her gaze to Thom, who was leaning into Mario. (That was a development.) Jorge was taking considered and thorough glances at them all, in order. She wasn't sure, but he seemed to be talking to himself—or into a recorder. Forsythe, the man of the hour and *Time* magazine's Man of the Year, had a long rich arm around Davis while listening to Steve expound on illegal moon immigration. Everyone else just drank. Except Jack, who, like Anne, was staring at Max. She smiled back at him. He raised his glass.

Later, over a "pudding," Forsythe walked the table, stopping to chat with each and every guest. He'd not buttoned his top shirt button, showing off his compression suit neckline. A real space cowboy.

"So are you liking your journey with us, Mrs. Whitshaw?"

Max nodded. "Max, please. Thank you so much for the opportunity. It's amazing."

"A small word for all this," Forsythe said, his hand moving again to the inner music that accompanied him. "Opportunity, that is."

"Well, I mean, privilege, I guess."

He smiled, beatific and lofty. "You're a lovely part of our puzzle."

Max sat up a bit, almost reaching out to grab him so he'd explain the word puzzle (no hand gesture with that), but Davis walked over, whispered in his ear, and Forsythe cleared his throat.

"I'm needed at control, my dear guests. I'll see you tomorrow in the atrium. Please don't hesitate to ask the staff for your every need."

Max remembered a line from *Jurassic Park*: "'We spared no expense.'"

That hadn't gone as planned, had it?

Then Davis whisked him away. Max sat back, looked at all these people, all of them powerful. But it would only take one solar wind or an alien blast or a surge of cosmic junk and they wouldn't be running from velociraptors but would be Sandra Bullock in *Gravity* without George Clooney to save them. No, they'd float away, cracking into shards of ice. Gone. All this money, all this power. *Poof!*

"Why do you think I won the lottery?" she asked Jack later as he sat on the edge of her bed, pulling on his nifty space station pajamas.

Jack shrugged, a classic good boy shrug, the kind he'd learned growing up in Manhattan and the Hamptons. At Phillips Exeter Academy and then Harvard. And now, at his family's investment firm, where he really didn't need to work, the family fortune built on the backs of all the people who ever earned a dollar in the United States.

"He said I was part of a puzzle."

Jack laughed, stood. "Aren't we all?"

"Even here?"

"More here."

"Well, it won't last."

Jack turned and looked at her, hands on his perfect hips. "Nothing does. Soon enough, we'll be home. The moon will just be the moon again."

But wasn't the moon supposed to be the moon, Max wondered? Wasn't home *home*?

The lack of gravity got to everyone. Standing, but not. Blood circulating, but more slowly. Up sometimes seemed down. Arms moved in ways that seemed a surprise. Max studied Steve's hand for a time, thinking it was hers. Organ failure would be in the cards for anyone staying too long. Forsythe seemed to be floating. Around the bright atrium, his laughter was like the clouds that were painted on the domed ceiling. In the corners, the guests were acting out a Roman orgy, feasting and kissing and walking off to their rooms in various couplings. Max felt her brain, at least most of it, cease working. Beyond any jetlag she'd ever experienced, she felt drugged and wondered if this were all just some bad LSD trip. In Jorge's or Anne's arms (wow, check that off the list), she found it hard to keep track of her own movements, her pleasure like the soundtrack from a TV show on in a faraway room.

Back in the dining area for their last meal, she finally saw it. The puzzle that she was a part of. Forsythe waved his hands, moving them all the way he wanted to. The true father of the mission, he'd put this person and that person and all the people at the table.

They acted to his whim, this multi-billion dollar extravaganza, a Versailles in the middle of the moon's desolation. Rome could burn and they would never feel it. As long as there were ions to fuel the shuttle and solar panels and exercise bikes, Forsythe might not ever have to go home and be among non-Forsythe-organized humans again.

"Good night," someone whispered to her later. A voice near her ear. Bruce? Steve? But the voice was familiar, old, known. She reached out to grab him—it was a him—but by the time her hand was out and searching, she was asleep.

In her seat, strapped down and encased in her suit, Max watched the pockmarked surface of the moon smooth in the distance, shining bright. Her heart beat in her throat, and she swallowed down what felt like brightness, the light pulsing in her chest. Turning a little, she saw the Earth in the far away distance. All she could ever really do, or be, was on that speck. Forsythe might think that there was life away from the planet, and maybe in some other century there would be. He could wave his magic wand, but there would be no magic. No music. All they'd done these past days was bring all their earth shit up to the moon and deal with it. She'd been with the rich and the famous and the smart, and when it came down to all the nothing around them, they were nothing. No amount of sex—especially the kind Max barely remembered—could make them more human. More real. Nothing they'd done in the shuttle or Moon Unit was more than flailing. They were inconsequential. Specks. Dots. Periods. Commas. Apostrophes. Sand. Lint. Dust. Dust and more dust.

On the blue and white planet where they'd lived their whole lives, though, they were people. Connected. Whole and true and terribly broken. But whole and home.

Reaching over across the seats, she grabbed Bruce's mitted hand, large and heavy and cumbersome. But solid. True. The real lottery of infinitesimal atmosphere, that tiny skin giving them all a chance.

Max squeezed Bruce as she stared through the darkness that stretched between the shuttle and earth; through the swirl of cloud, light blue, indigo, forest greens, browns of every shade, down through the sky to the ground, into her very house, into the brightness of things. All her precious gifts—her father's baton tucked safely in her underwear drawer, her wedding ring in the clam shell on the bathroom counter, her coffee mug by her computer and manuscripts. Her people. Her husband and children, asleep in their beds. There she would be. There. That was the red arrow on the poster. There. She was there.

A Miracle, Really

The first time, Dorie was fifty feet away as the kid spun around the blind corner, his shiny, silver Mercedes drifting on two wheels, at least for a second. Sun glinted through the sudden spaces under the car. The *For Sale* sign in front of the Delgado's house rocked back and forth. Wind blew dried eucalyptus leaves, the edges thin as knives.

She threw up her arms as the car righted itself, the leash yanking Remy, her dog. Remy whined. The kid skidded hard to a stop, the rear of his car lifting. The smell of hot brakes and tires wafted from under the car as the motor ran.

"What the hell!" she yelled, ignoring the bang of her heart.

The car inched closer, and when he was two feet away, he unrolled his window. The first thing she noted were his pimples, and then the shine of grease on his forehead. Might as well wear a sign that read *Hormones* she thought. He smelled like gels and cigarettes smoked by friends in the back seat.

"Sorry."

"Sorry?" she said. "I was just about at that turn. Any closer, my dog and I would have been dead."

He put on a sullen face, eyes glazed and staring straight ahead.

"You should drive ten miles an hour on this street. It's basically one lane. Do you want to run over someone?"

He pushed a hand through his thick dark hair. Then he shrugged, and for the thousandth time, Dorie marveled that the entire population hadn't been killed by teenaged boys. Her own hadn't managed to kill her, and they'd lived in her house.

"I don't really feel like talking with your mother. Tina, right? But I will. Slow the hell down."

To his credit, he looked her in the eyes, dark brown-eyed, white-toothed, at least two good attributes. He'd probably been an adorable toddler, staggering around the house on chubby legs and with a big smile. Poor kid. Driving was likely his only power, she thought. But still.

"Sorry," he said.

"You said that already."

Sullen again. A car pulled up behind him, the driver tapping on the horn.

"Okay." She stepped back and let him pass, Remy close at her side. "Don't do it again."

She and Remy walked on, Dorie kicking at crushed pine cones. Asshole, she thought, her word for people who did things wrong. And most everyone up in the Oakland Hills did. Driving was the most obvious, the most egregious, drivers barreling down the skinny, mountainous roads at forty miles an hour, straddling the double-yellow lines or just ignoring them, texting and making calls and yelling at their kids. They slid through stop signs and lights, whipped around corners. They drank big cups of Starbucks coffee and held onto the wheel with slack left hands.

Walkers—dog walkers—weren't much better, letting dogs off-leash, dogs that were supposedly "friendly." The ones that "never bite" or have "never done that before." Right, Dorie thought, saving Remy weekly from snapping, slavering biters. Or the walkers were just benignly oblivious, using expandable leashes, their dogs crisscrossing the street so that it was impossible for Dorie to know which side to stay on. Then there were the ones that didn't pick up the mounds of dog shit, piles of it everywhere. Or the ones who left the full poo bags on the street. Who did they think was going to clean up after them?

She didn't even want to contemplate about the bicyclists zipping down from the regional parks. Toward the end of their marriage, her ex-husband Dan took up biking. A two-thousand dollar technological marvel bike, special shoes, fancy helmet. All that damp, smelly Spandex. On weekends, he'd leave for the entire day, riding from Oakland, through Berkeley, into Contra Costa County and the wide-open suburbs with their trails or, at least, wider streets.

Or so he said.

Now, half the time, Dorie had the notion of ramming bikers and flipping them up like poker chips. But instead, she was forced to follow them down the hill, looking at their ghastly-ass cracks through their worn-out biking shorts.

But really, no one should live up here at all. The 1991 fire hadn't taught any of them a lesson. Big houses built one after the other next to stands of drought-dry eucalyptus and now-dying Monterey pines. Empty lots let go to seed. Clumps of oily, invasive Scotch broom. Budget cuts and closed fire stations. Small streets, barely big enough for the remaining fire engines. Global warming. Offshore flows. This entire hilly community was one struck match away from extinction. Just like this neighbor kid, people were blind to anyone but themselves.

But who was she fooling? Despite the danger, she and Dan had moved to the hills for the view; for the neighbors with kids, the block parties, the nearby parks, the swim club. Now Dorie was the only one left in the big house, rolling around it like a marble in a matchbox.

Back at home, Dorie took off Remy's leash and gave him his dried bull's penis, marketed as a Bully Stick dog chew. He trotted outside to his spot on the outdoor couch and started gnawing.

Sitting down at the kitchen counter, she clicked onto her laptop searching the neighborhood watch list for Tina Simmons' email address. After what Dorie saw today, it was clear Tina needed a new script. What kind of advice was she giving that monster? From what Dorie had gathered at block parties, the father wasn't around and hadn't been for years. It must have been Tina that taught her son to drive like a maniac.

Dorie scrolled through, finding Tina's name and address. Settling in her chair, Dorie clicked and started writing, but then she sat back and stared at Remy in the sun, the dog oblivious to bad parenting and near-death experiences.

How many times had Dorie's older son Robert driven while drunk? Or while on some other substance, a fact Dorie would only learn about years later? He'd sneak out of the house, first to run around the neighborhood with his friends, and then later to drive like an idiot, lights off. He'd siphon gas from Dorie's and Dan's cars, speed around until he ran out, and then steal more gas from someone else. Robert and his friends destroyed the local soccer field and had to do community service for weeks at the nearby assisted living facility. He was lucky Dan pulled a few lawyer strings and kept him out of juvenile hall.

Dorie clicked on "to" and then "subject," writing *Your Son.*

She sat back. *Her sons.* Robert, okay now. And Will, just into his life, almost independent at twenty-seven, a firefighter recently hired to a district. Finally. All she paid for was his health insurance and his phone. A miracle, really. He hadn't learned to read until halfway through second-grade, even though Dorie and Dan knew he was smart. Then there were those disturbing drawings in third grade. The bombs and blood. That black and red ink. All the meetings with teachers as exhausted as Dorie was at her own school district, with her own students and their hyper parents. Twenty-two years of it. It was endless. The forms. The Individual Education

Program plans. The teacher notes home, the calls, the after-school check-ins.

Being a teacher hadn't made it any easier to be a parent. How she and Will wrangled about homework, both of them red-eyed, wild-haired by night's end. The pages of reading. The long essays. How he'd stalk off, slamming doors, his eyes averted when he slunk into the kitchen in the morning, submitting to the daily routine. His stiff, battle-ready back as he walked out the front door, hefting his fifty-pound backpack. If it hadn't been for the resource room (special education) and the therapists (for the whole family) Dorie might be making weekly visits to Lompoc prison with all the other mothers and wives.

Will probably didn't even remember half of it. Or that she'd been there the whole time, standing behind him.

Dorie glanced back at Remy, his black eyes on her as he chewed. So much better to have a dog. You could screw up and dogs forgot. You could do your worst, and they still loved you. You could fill a bowl of water with an old garden hose. You could feed them hard pellets of food. You could lock them in a cage for four hours with only a rawhide bone and a blanket and all was forgiven.

Dorie sighed, closed down her email, and shut her laptop.

She woke up, something covering her eyes, maybe her whole head—her body immobilized, the world muffled. Dorie licked her lips. The warm air around her was filled with noises but empty of anything she understood enough to hear.

"Water," she said.

Water appeared, a straw on her lips. She sucked but couldn't see who held the glass.

She released the straw, sank back, but even that tiny movement seemed impossible. The tendons on the sides of her neck pulsed and burned. Each vertebrae of her spine screamed on the stiff mattress.

"Where?" she asked.

Then there was a muffled blur, an itchy scratch of sound, and she could hear. She breathed in hospital—bleached cotton, isopropyl alcohol, her own body, a kind of dead skin cast smell she remembered from when she broke her arm in second grade—but she didn't know which hospital (Highland? God. Kaiser? Lord). Or who was with her. Robert was in Berlin fomenting political change, and Will was in the Cascades of Washington State, fighting wildland fires. Dan? Dan had left years ago, so—

"My dog!" She thought to sit up, but tubes, wires, and her own body constrained her. A hand steadied her on the bed.

"He's fine, I promise," the somehow familiar voice said. Dorie turned toward it, her, but her eyes were still covered, the world a vague yellow. "We're taking care of him."

Dorie let her heart calm. She felt someone tugging the blanket around her shoulders. As she exhaled, she focused on finding her body. Closing her eyes against the yellow (something oily covering them) she searched out her right foot. There it was at the end of the bed. And then her left. She tried to wiggle her toes, and she might have, but there was pain, something that radiated up her legs into her dead center, which felt achy and deep, a well of blood, maroon, glistening.

But other than that, she felt okay, her normal feeling from chest to fingertips. She moved those, too, scratching the sheet as she did.

"What happened?" she asked.

"You don't remember?" a second voice asked.

A slash of sun on Remy's white fluffy fur. A click of dog tags. A pine cone, a scrap of paper. A sound, like thick packing tape ripped fast and hard off cardboard. Then something she could not really describe, not even now that it was over: a bump, her body screaming and flying. A wrench in her arm, her whole side, a crack of spine and skull, a hard white flash.

Then she was here.

That little shit.

She breathed in and held it, trying to see the car as it smashed into her, the hard wing of his front bumper, the bull of his grill as it wanged into her torso.

Maybe she was inventing this part, but she imagined his wide eyes full of terror.

"Dammit," Dorie whispered.

"He didn't mean to," the first voice said, Dorie starting to remember where she'd heard it before.

"Shhh," the second voice said, clearly in charge. A nurse. "Let her rest."

Dorie thought of the t-shirt a man at the gym wore daily: *I'll rest when I'm dead.*

She could hear and feel. She could move her toes.

"He hit me," she said to the voices.

"He didn't mean to," the familiar first voice repeated.

"I warned him," Dorie said.

"Didn't pay you or the law any mind," the nurse voice said.

There was a pause, whispers, hospital sounds in the hall. Dorie swallowed, her throat parched. "Am I all right?"

"Your doctor will be in to see you soon." The nurse moved close, adjusting things around Dorie's pillow, machines clicking and beeping.

"I know what that means," Dorie said, her words coming out of her mouth in whole, slow pieces. "I watch TV. I'm not paralyzed because I can move. See."

She wiggled her toes again. Then she moved her fingers, and that was when she noticed the casts.

"My arms?"

The familiar voice was crying now, and if Dorie weren't in casts, she'd slap her. Who was she, anyway, worrying so much about the "he" who hit her? Why did she care some much? Why was she defending this stupid ignorant kid who didn't listen? Why was she sitting next to Dorie instead of Robert or Will? What about Dorie's friends and family, her sister and cousins?

And then she knew. Tina.

"It's all your fault," Dorie whispered.

"I know," Tina sobbed back. "I know."

The news wasn't as bad as the television show she watched on Thursday nights would have made it, no paralysis from the waist down, no surprise brain tumor along with the concussion or incipient MS, exacerbated by stress. The show would have included emotional visits from her mother, admitting finally that Dorie was adopted or a child of rape. This fine episode would have had her sons calling from the tops of mountains or from small submarines at the deepest ocean depths. The doctors would plead for them to get to the hospital without delay. They would hurl themselves home, bringing gifts and their hearts on platters. They would have kneeled at her bedside and forgiven her all her mothering mistakes, handing back her wrong words and moves in brown paper bags she could throw away. Possibly, her ex would have seen the errors of his ways, leaving his young bride for the true comforts of the good woman he'd spent half his life with.

But Dorie only had two fractured arms (apparently she flung them upon impact, trying to protect herself), a concussion, scratched corneas, and random lacerations from rocks and branches, tossed as she was onto the steep hillside. They were still watching for internal bleeding. She would feel this way for a long time.

According to Tina, smart Remy dodged and avoided collision. He hadn't run away, either. Remy waited by Dorie's side until the paramedics came, went placidly with Tina after the ambulance roared off. Now according to Tina, the shitty murderous driving kid was dog-sitting and dog-walking and being very helpful.

"Steven has a good heart," Tina said, again, but for the first time today, day four of Dorie's hospital stay. Dorie's arms were elevated on pillows, and she had strict instructions to avoid movement, which meant that the nurses came in with a bedpan when necessary. Tomorrow, though, she was to be moved to a convalescent facility where she would actually convalesce. Her eye bandages would come off later today. Even better, the nurses promised her a sponge bath before bed.

"Really? Again?" Dorie said. "I don't want to talk about it anymore."

"He's a good boy."

"Good? What's that even mean?"

"He stays with me." Tina's voice was almost a wail. "Good that way."

"Right." Dorie turned to the wall before remembering that with the gauze, no one could see her cry.

Go home, she wanted to shout. *Get the hell out of here.*

"It's Steven's father." Tina said. Dorie heard rustling tissue and the blowing of a nose.

"It's always the father," Dorie said, though it wasn't. On bad days, she worried she was the dark heart of her sons' faults, personality quirks and moral lapses. Sometimes when she couldn't sleep, she ran through her litany of errors: antibiotics, hot sauna, sex, glass of wine while pregnant, inability to say no, inclination to yell, general and persistent fatigue during their childhoods. Too much imagination (all those trips to tide pools and the hollowed out redwood trees and the jellybean and salt water taffy factories) and too little (wanting them to play sports and take dance lessons).

"He left us both," Tina said.

"Join the club," Dorie said. "But my boys don't drive forty miles an hour around blind turns on tiny roads."

"He didn't mean to," Tina whined. Dorie hadn't seen Tina for a couple of years, not since that last neighborhood barbeque. After-noon breeze blowing Tina's dyed red hair, brown and gray roots. Too much laughter for too little happening, a clutched glass of white wine in her hand, skin pale and brittle and too much of it exposed in that black t-shirt. Looking over her head for someone to what? Come up to her? To tell her that her suspicions were right. She'd made every possible mistake and would continue to do so. Tina's whole life? A failure.

Tina sniffed, the wet sound of her rubbing her nose. "He really didn't mean to. It wasn't on purpose."

More tissue, more blowing.

What was the definition of *mean to* anyway? There was the attempt to do something—drive fast—and the outcome. Steven could just have easily ended up at home, parked in his own garage. He might have slammed into the kitchen, kissed Tina on the cheek and asked what was for dinner. Instead of breaking bits of Dorie's body, he might have played video games and then told his mother stories about water polo practice over dinner. He didn't mean to bang her up into the air. Dorie didn't mean to be in that exact spot at that moment, waiting to be split like kindling.

"I'm going to drop the charges." Dorie said, as if this plan had been approved by her lawyer and accountant.

Tina stilled. "What are you going to do?"

"I'm going to sue you for your umbrella policy. That and the car insurance."

Tina's gasp stabbed the air.

"And?"

"You're going to take that car away. He's got to walk or get a ride."

After the drugs and the soccer field incident, Robert took the bus everywhere. Finding rides home from the movies and dances and football games. Girlfriends driving him home after parties.

Long after Robert left for college, Will clung to rules not made for him. He never received a warning, much less a speeding ticket, his body stiff and hyperaware in the driver seat. Just last year when he picked her up from the SeaTac airport, Dorie patted his shoulder as he merged onto the highway, hoping to feel his bones and muscles sag under her cupped palm. But he stayed tense, every part of him still afraid, as if he believed that at any moment he would start making his brother's mistakes.

"Anything else?" Tina asked.

Something swung in Dorie's mind, an idea she grabbed onto.

"I'm going to collect the money and move."

Tina inhaled. Dorie surprised herself with a smile, feeling the stiffness of the pillowcase against her cheek. She flexed her foot, her hand. She felt the healed parts of her deep insides. "I am going to move."

Tina breathed out and then settled against the chair.

She was quiet for so long that Dorie found herself falling asleep behind her gauze. She dreamed about her sons. Not the way they were now, all grown up and far away. Not the men they'd become with women who had naturally taken Dorie's place. And not the long-boned, big-fisted, baby-faced teenaged boys to whom she'd fed plates and plates of food.

Not the boys who sat with her in movie theatres, science-fiction blasting bright on the screen, their eyes filling with story. Not even the grammar school boys with their lunch boxes and bad jokes, jabbering on the way home from school about who farted at recess.

No, in her dream Robert and Will were little again, curly-haired and wet from the bath. Their skin shiny and slick, their bodies smooth, perfect, and round. White smiles. Red bow lips. She could feel them against her body, warm from the bath, wrapped in a towel, pressing their faces against her neck. They were it. They were the only reason she was here on the planet. The well of them filled her. All her failures and hopes and mistakes broke away, her face full with a smile that yanked on her bandages. Dorie tried to ignore the pull of tape, but she came back to the room and heard Tina still next to her, sniffling.

"Thank you," Tina said.

Dorie waited for the sound of her butt lifting from the chair, heels clacking, the sound of Tina walking away from her responsibility. But there were only sniffles, the *whiff whiff* of the tissues yanked from the box.

By the time she'd been transferred to Apple Valley Convalescent Facility, Dorie's sight had returned, though she wished it hadn't. Oh, for the gauze, she thought, gazing down her body, the sticks of her legs, the T of her set arms. She did not want a mirror, but she felt the shape of her hair, tangled around her head, dirty, needing a dye job, a week past due. Gray roots for sure. Or maybe she'd stop all that now. Thirty years of chemicals on her scalp had been enough. She was scared to think about her toenails and had not asked for anyone to take off her hospital socks. The action was slower here than the hospital, less urgent, the end for so many of the patients known. Some would get better, some not. But everything was going to take time.

The buildings fanned out over the campus, surrounded by water, trees, tended lawns. She was too well acquainted with the soccer field next door, the one Robert ripped to shreds with his used Infiniti, he and that mad bunch with their beer cans and joints. Afterward, the new sod replaced, the green soared all the way up to Apple Valley and its smooth asphalt traffic circle and stately trees.

Every day, a doctor came to check on her, as did a physical therapist, an older woman named Anne, who barely smiled but moved Dorie around the bed, worked her legs, her shoulders, massaged away the tense knot of headache where her skull met her neck. She thought to tell Anne about her plans to move. First, the casts would have to go. Then the house. And the job. But under all the plans and details lived something else, a tingly feeling she couldn't name.

"I'm moving soon," Dorie told Anne during one of her last sessions.

Anne looked down at her, one of Dorie's cast arms in her hands. She reached up to Dorie's shoulder, feeling muscle, her fingers strong.

"I hate change," she said, gently lifting Dorie to a sitting position. "But sometimes, there's nothing you can do about it."

Then Anne went back to her work. Dorie's body. Her body. The work of so many people. They all came in for something. The squeeze of the blood pressure band, tight above her cast. The beep of the thermometer. The slap of plastic food tray on plastic bed tray.

Her boys checked in. Her mother called from her own assisted living facility every other day to parse the extent of Dorie's injuries, the physical therapy treatment plan, the disability benefits. Three friends from work arrived with plants and candy and gossip about which teachers were retiring at the end of the term. The kids were acting up. Recess had been cancelled three times last week. The big news? Someone stole the copy card. Get well notes slipped in from neighbors and old college pals living in other states and countries. But mostly it was just Tina and her, rain beating on the windows in the afternoon, the snores of her roommate with the two knee replacements punctuating the stale air. Tina had stopped defending her son. They passed the days watching television or reading from a local paper that Tina brought in. They laughed about the police blotter from Piedmont, the enclave tucked into Oakland like an ancient walled city: *Dead squirrel found in yard. Officer called* and *Man knocking on doors without permit* and *Large bag discovered on sidewalk.*

Outside, willow branches swayed.

Two weeks later, Dorie was sitting on the edge of her bed, her re-casted arms in slings. A cab was coming for her, an attendant hired from the online service awaiting her arrival at home. Her lawyer filled in all the insurance claim forms, the money soon to be wired into her account. Dorie had her mind on a particular real estate agent, and part of her occupational therapy was working on a computer. Mindless activity to occupy her when all she could do was tap, tap, tap.

She searched for somewhere flat. Somewhere with big streets and sidewalks. Somewhere with dog parks. Sonoma. Marin. Napa. Mendocino. San Diego. Maui and Oahu on the back burner. Maybe not the back burner. Why worry about her children visiting her when they haven't done so here? The neighborhood? Teaching? She'd let it go as if it were a blanket, a throw, a half completed afghan, crochet hook skittering across the floor. She'd pick up what was left of her old life and flick it, let it billow up once, twice, and then let it drift away.

A man walked down the hall, and she imagined it was the cab driver, but then there *he* was, in the doorway. Steven.

Dorie stared, expecting to see Tina slump down the hallway after him, but he was alone.

"Why are you here?"

"God," he said. His misery glowed.

Dorie struggled to speak, as if something were hitched on her vocal cords. It rested there on her larynx, her howl. Her yell at him about how he'd wrecked her daily routine. Her orderly fashion. Her to and fro. How he'd broken the solid circle of her solitary life she'd bent into place after Dan left. How dare he! How dare he!

But how dare he not? How dare he not live, all those impulses inside him?

They stared at each other. Dorie watched the beat of his breath in his throat.

"Here, help me up," she said.

He plodded toward her, his mouth turned down, eyes solemn. He was so tall, all arms and legs, his body stretched out like a plank. He was a flicker away from being a man, off into the life that would take him away.

"I'm so sorry." He reached out for her arm and then flinched when he touched her cast, his hand inching toward her shoulder. Dorie leaned forward like the physical therapist showed her, planted her feet and used her quads.

"Do you need a wheelchair?"

"Don't want it," Dorie said. "Let's get out of there before they catch me."

Steven glanced at her, his eyes wide, lips pressed together, but his step matched hers.

"You drive too fast," she said, as they shuffled out of the room, Steven picked up her bag and slung it on a shoulder.

"It was a stupid game. I tried to see how high I could jump the car. That time you caught me, I swore I wouldn't do it again."

"But you did," Dorie nodded to a couple of the patients she'd spoken to during her stay.

"My mom took away the car," he said, holding onto her so gently, she thought she could feel his pulse through his fingers. "I'm not going to drive again for a year."

"How did you get here?"

"Mom called a cab," he said.

Dorie let him steady her as they walked down the hall, past the nurses, the squat receptionist, the other patients lined up like wheelchair soldiers in the dayroom. Steven was taller than both Will and Robert, his gait lope-y, his arms long, hands and fingers thin and pale. But he smelled like they used to. Soap, thick white patches of deodorant under each arm, undeterred hope with a layer of fear, the tang of arrogance, the surety that he would never die. Walking with him down the hall began to feel familiar, so much so that she almost pressed her head against Steven's chest, even though his thin bony rib cage wouldn't feel the same as either of her sons'. But for one stride, two, she imagined it would.

Out in the air, Dorie blinked against the light and then saw the yellow cab, Remy in the back seat, his tail wagging.

Steven lowered her into the back seat, and as she sat down, Remy crawled into her lap.

"All set?" Steven said. "Ready?"

Dorie nodded, surprise tears as she put on her seatbelt. Remy licked her cheek, her ear. She wiped away the tears along with his saliva, his panting warm dog breath in her face.

The cab driver started the motor. In the seat next to her was the boy who plowed her down and smashed her flat, leaving her broken. As Steven talked to the cab driver, she thought him so far into the future that all of this was only memory. That lady and the dog. *The lady I hit with Mom's car. The lady who left and never came back.*

Dorie's breath was shallow. Her broken arms ached. Here she was again, smack in the moments that change everything. Robert before leaving the house for a night out with his drunken, noisy friends. Will before going to college. Even earlier. Dan before he got on his shiny new bike and rode all the way to a new wife.

The driver pulled into traffic, Remy's head in her lap.

"First semester senior year," he said, "I'm going to England. Study abroad."

"I guess you'll really be flying them. Jumping across the pond as they say," Dorie said, surprised again by the tightness in her throat. He wasn't her son leaving, but she thought of Tina, alone in her house with her tissues. "Will you be there for the holidays?" she asked.

He shrugged.

"Your mom could fly over. Do Boxing Day in London."

Steven petted Remy.

"Maybe."

Steven started telling her about school. His best class, chemistry. His mother, so worried all the time. He petted Remy some more, and then they looked out the windows, the air blowing through his dark hair, through Remy's fluff.

What was changing? Dorie didn't know. Her whole life? Nothing? It should feel bigger than this, wider than the small thing cracking open inside her as she sat in the backseat of the taxi. More than just hope, the same hope she felt in Steven as she clutched him in the hallway. There should be a clear outcome in sight. Nothing ambiguous. Something to interpret and understand. A big, *Oh, yes!* But all she knew for sure was that this pimply, gangly, and still growing boy smashed into her and flung her up. There she was caught by the heavy car, tossed skyward, arms out in front of her.

Shortcut Through the Alley

Harry Scott knows he shouldn't take the shortcut through the alley, the five o'clock Oakland morning too new to be safe. In the gray, half-light, every trash can hides an ominous humped figure. But he always makes the dash behind the rink because every morning he's late. Pulling his collar up around his neck, he cringes in anticipation of Mahmoud's ire and makes a quick right turn, arms crossed, head down, imagining the brittle crack of hypodermic needles under his work boots. His eyes on the pavement, he listens to his own heavy steps and the space around him, the skiff of gravel and the distant hum of the 980 freeway.

When he left the house this morning to catch the downtown bus, his daughter Amelia's bedroom door was closed. Harry stopped for a second, his hand shaped like the doorknob he should have grabbed and turned, but he didn't, knowing even as he walked away, she wasn't asleep in her twin bed. Her absence had a texture Harry could feel and taste, a chilled spoon, a dirty knife.

Now, he knows he should have pushed in and flicked on the truth. But instead, he passed by, headed down the stairs, and walked into the bright yellow kitchen where his wife Inez was cooking eggs and bacon.

Later, he will call home. Harry will go back to the landing in front of his daughter's door. He will turn the knob.

But now, he hugs himself against the thick marine layer, exhales, and then, there's something: A mew, a plastic whir, a mew.

Rustling. A pause of nothing but static. Harry's heart speeds and lurches, and he stops, glances toward the dark slice of alley wall, sees the full garbage cans and then hears it again, a sound as soft as first breath.

He's late, the ice will harden and then melt, Mahmoud will yell and carry on, but Harry takes three steps to the garbage can, pushes aside a paper bag and then uses it to move an old towel, a wadded jacket, an empty bottle. Behind the mess is a black plastic bag. He waits, hoping for nothing. Large rat. Or a cat. A yowl and dart, tail up, fur raised. He will laugh, go to work, and nod through Mahmoud's tirade.

But like all bad things, this one happens on schedule. The bag rustles. Whatever is inside mews, but it's no mew. A tiny, surprised cry. Harry understands this is a bag you don't open, much less pick up. Which he does, the top of the ruffled plastic fluttering over his fist like dry hair, the moving heft of its contents pulling on his arm.

By weight and sound and the specific quivers of the plastic, Harry knows what is in the bag and now he has no choice but to open it. He doesn't want to, but he rests the bag on the pavement, and pulls open the knotted top and squints into the darkness.

"Oh, Jesus have mercy," he cries, his hands scuttling in the bag, grabbing onto and lifting up red, crinkled skin.

The baby is tiny and frail, but it's—she's—breathing, even though someone (*who for goddamn's sake?*) has stuffed yellow tissue in her mouth. He digs it out from between her tiny lips and reminds himself to check for a heartbeat, his hairy head resting on this new, wet flesh, smelling blood, hair, and unnamed odors of mother and child.

He unzips his jacket and puts the baby next to his shirt, zipping his body to hers, picking up the bag and the tissue, and then running to Mel's Coffee Shop, knowing that someone will know what to do.

Later, in the police station, the sergeant gives him the once over.

"So, you were walking down the alley. At five o'clock a.m.? You say. . .Oh, here. . .You work in the ice rink?"

"I drive the Zamboni. I get there before the skaters. Practice and all."

"Every morning?"

"Except Saturdays and Sundays. Days off. Union."

The sergeant nods, snorting into his notes. "Say no more, my friend. If we have any further questions, we'll call. This your work number? Seven oh six nine four three six? Cell or work?"

Harry tells him work and stands up, clutching his hat and thermos. Briefly, he wonders if his coffee is still warm and taps the aluminum cylinder against his Levis.

"What about her? Will she be okay?" he asks.

"That'll be the doctors' jobs. And then, God willing, the social workers'. Here is the hospital's number. Or you can call us for an update if you want, though I'm sure you have better things to do."

The cop looks up over his reading glasses at Harry, a gaze constant and smart, as if the guy thinks Harry might have actually left the baby there himself.

Outside, the sky has opened into blue, sunlight glinting off the Federal Building like two triangular eyes. The downtown police station isn't far from the rink, so Harry walks back to work, swinging his thermos, his eyes on the cracked pavement. He tries to forget the baby, but he begins to feel his body swinging to the rhythm of the bag just before he opened it. The sad fact of it was he'd swung it like a cradle, back and forth, the same rhythm he'd used to push Amelia in her bassinet, slowly, lulling her into sleep, or just pushed, watching her brown eyes watching him, hooking one huge finger in her tiny hand.

Where is that baby? Where did she go? Where is the little girl he brought to the ice rink, holding her hand as he convinced her to let go of the wall and take his hand. Harry can still see Amelia in her red sweater and white knitted hat, her amazed smile as she slid skated toward him in her tiny ice skates, her hands outstretched.

What year did Amelia leave him, both him and Inez, and go into her own life? What was the exact day and time Harry should have grabbed her and held her back? Should he have moved his family to the suburbs, where the music and boys and parties seemed less threatening or at least not as loud? Amelia's boyfriends drove cars that blasted loud music and wore pants that were strapped around their thighs with slim, tight belts. One had a gold tooth, another wore a thick necklace and a baseball cap in such a stupid angle that Harry wanted to flip it off his stupid head.

And now there's Ef. Ef all day, and, it seems, all night.

"Where in the hell have you been, Har-ry? The skaters, they come and they go. They are all complaining about the ice. Rough, they say. They give me the bad looks." Mahmoud, the pro and manager, stands behind the ice skate rental counter, counting out pairs of figure skates.

"I couldn't really call. They were asking me a lot of questions."

Mahmoud shakes his head. "Who are they who ask these questions? What is going on?"

"Police," Harry says, opening his thermos, a thin steam stream whisking out the top. "I found a baby. In the alley. Behind the rink."

Mahmoud looks up at him over the neatly lined up skates, the white and black tongues as open as his mouth. "A baby. I am not believing this."

Harry takes a sip of coffee that Inez brewed this morning before she went to her job at the Del Monte canning plant. She has worked with vegetables for eighteen years, sorting them by feel, her quick fingers yanking out browning tomatoes and yellowed string beans, her hands then gliding smoothly back to the conveyor belt, searching for more imperfections.

And even though she washes and scrubs her hands and hair and face, everything about her smells like the tinny insides of cans, the spicy, sharp liquids for chilies, peppers, and pickles, and hot, salty water. Now, as Harry breathes in the coffee, he can taste a lick of orange carrot on the rim of his cup.

"I put her under my jacket and ran to Mel's and called the police. They came and then the ambulance came, and they took the baby away. She's alive. At least when I last saw her."

Mahmoud throws up his hands, a single black skate tumbling to the rubber matted floor. "This city I am not liking. Murders. Robberies. Bad city management. Can't even help us to find the funding. And now, babies in the alley." Mahmoud clomps off to his office, the laces of his skates dragging behind him.

Harry swallows down his coffee, then goes to the break room. He opens his locker, hanging up his jacket and setting down the thermos. He takes out the blue wool shirt he uses while driving the Zamboni and working on the boiler and plumbing, his name scrawled on the left breast pocket in red, the *y* dipping down and underlining the rest of the letters. Using the small mirror in the locker, Harry whisks a comb through his thick dark hair.

"It makes you look dignified," said Inez. "Forget the commercials. At your age, no one would believe you weren't going gray anyway. Look at the rest of us!"

Inez laughed and undid her hairclip, her long black hair swishing across her back, gray creeping down from her crown like frost.

Harry can almost feel Inez's hair in his palms now, but then he remembers the baby, its thin black hair hugging its scalp like moss, the blue veined umbilical cord wrapped around its feet and legs, both eyes (*What color?*) squeezed shut.

Even though he knows Inez won't be home until noon and that Amelia should be at school, he calls home. While he waits for the answering machine to click on, Harry conjures how he will hurt Ef if he's done anything to Amelia. When Harry first met Ef, his impulse was to crack him a good one, jaw, nose, sharp, thin shoulder. Just the sight of the boy—bony and dark with straight black hair and a silver stud in his eyebrow—set Harry's teeth on edge. But Inez said, "At least we know where she is when she isn't here. Do you know what other mothers tell me? Drugs? Pregnancy? Stealing? Maria Jackson said her daughter took the three hundred dollars she kept under the rug for emergencies and spent it on a leather jacket. And then wore it home! So, Amelia is out late, so she sleeps over there at night. Be thankful is what I'm saying."

Harry still feels his arm stiffen when Ef is in their house, sitting there like he owns the place, watching something on Netflix, and curling his long arms around his daughter. And Harry sighs when he sees a new piercing on Amelia: ears, nose, navel, god knows what else. Harry shivers at the thoughts of steel through soft flesh, his mouth dry. He almost turns and leaves the house when he hears the music, not the music of his youth where he could hear the words—*Black Water* by The Doobie Brothers or *Stairway to Heaven* by Led Zepplin—not even the mariachi music of Inez's family, but sad, twisted notes that make Harry want to cry because he doesn't understand why Ef and Amelia want to fill their lives with drumbeats of pain. What he wants to do is run to them both and say, "This is what we are trying to forget. Don't you understand?"

But Harry never says anything; instead, he walks silently through his house, past the living room, the smell of clove cigarettes, and the sounds of loud, desperate voices on the TV. He knows if he stops, looks at their bodies twisted together on the couch, all baggy pants and huge t-shirts, Amelia's eyes lined with so much black she looks ill or beaten, he will say the wrong thing or yell or hit the wall. So he walks to the kitchen, closes his eyes to the afternoon sun coming through the back window, holds Inez around her waist as she cooks dinner, bending his mouth to her hair, breathing in lima beans, peas, whole kernels of yellow hominy.

When the nine o'clock skaters leave the ice, Harry warms up the Zamboni and listens to the engine, slapping his gloved hands together as he waits, cracking his knuckles, blowing out puffs of frozen breath. After a few minutes, Harry gives the okay for Mahmoud to open the automatic doors and sound the buzzer. Sliding the machine out on the ice, he makes the first wide circle, watching the ice sluice out flat, frozen, and clean behind him. He winds closer to the middle of the rink, each oval smaller and smaller until there is just one bumpy strip in the middle like a giant slit eye. Some days, when Mahmoud isn't here, he leaves it, even though the really good skaters work out there, practicing their lifts and jumps and throws. But, he thinks, it is only a small line, and he likes the way it looks as he parks the Zamboni and turns around, the eye watching him from a sea of glass.

"Har-ry. The phone, it is for you," Mahmoud says.

Harry picks up the phone in the break room. "Hello?" he says, thinking it might be the police, but it's Inez.

"Harry," she says, her voice far away, the sound of the machines and aluminum clatter in the background.

"Inez," he says. "I left a message at home. Did you get it? Did you hear what happened? I've had such a morning. I—"

"I didn't check. I'm calling about—"

"I've been at the police station for awhile—"

"Oh, my God? What has happened to her?"

"She's fine. She'll live. That's what the police think."

"Oh, *dios mio*! Amelia! I knew something had happened. What's wrong with my baby?"

"Amelia? No, Inez, not Amelia. Calm down. That's not, I mean, I'm not talking about Amelia."

He hears Inez breathing, tears in her throat. "You scared me, Harry. Honestly! Listen, The school called about Amelia. She didn't go to school again. What is this? The fifth time this month? Anyway. I just wanted to know if you'd talked to her. . .But what are you talking about? Who is *she*?"

Harry sighs. "I found a baby behind the rink."

"A baby?"

"I went to the police station. The baby is at the hospital."

"Oh," says Inez, her voice lighter because now the *she* is not Amelia, *she* belongs to someone else and is someone else's problem. *She* is not theirs. "Oh, Harry. That's terrible. Poor baby."

"She was in a Hefty bag. There was still blood on her. Someone tried to kill her, I guess. But they didn't try very hard because she was still breathing."

Inez gasps and, behind her, the sounds of her co-workers, the clanking of machines, hard hats, cans, levers, heat, steam. "Oh, my. Harry—I've got to go. But we've got to find Amelia. I called Ef, but he doesn't answer either. Call me if you hear anything."

Harry hangs up the phone and digs in his back pocket for his cell phone and all his contacts. He calls the high school and gets a busy signal, but instead of hanging up right away, he listens to the steady electric thwanging, thinking of a night almost one month ago when Inez was visiting her sister Lola in Hayward, his dinner wrapped in tight foil packets when he came home from work.

"Amelia," he called into the living room. "Are you hungry? Amelia? Is Ef there, too?"

She didn't answer, but eventually he heard the angry throb of the music stop and then the fabric shuffle of her walk, her pants dragging around her feet as she walked down the hall. When she came into the kitchen, he smiled, peeling off the foil from two steaks, baked potatoes, a green salad with ranch dressing.

"Mom made dinner," he said looking at her, knowing before he met her eyes that she was rolling them upward, titling her head almost to the ceiling, throwing her long hair behind one shoulder, looking, he imagined, for another father to materialize from the heavens or for some beam to take her away from him and the six long hours before her mother returned.

Sitting at the kitchen table, he watched her chew through her meat, her head bent forward, her hair looping on the table in coils. "Where's Ef tonight? I haven't seen him in a while," he said.

For a second, she glanced at him, her brown eyes alert within the pie of dark makeup, but then she must have remembered how Harry ignored them both, barely nodding to Ef even when the four of them would sit together at the dining room table.

"Don't know," she said finally, picking up the potato skin and putting it in her mouth, a small trickle of butter running down her chin.

She didn't say anything else, and while he could, Harry watched her eat, following the butter as it dripped on the table.

Now, Harry hangs up on the school's busy signal and rifles through another pocket for the hospital's number. Finally getting to the right department, he finds himself talking to a social worker.

"No. I'm not a relative. *I* found her. I found her by the ice rink. The police gave me this number."

"Really. What did you say your name was?"

Harry starts to answer, then hangs up, the phone receiver hot in his hands.

Later, outside on the curb, Harry eats a Polish dog from the snack truck. The dog is thick as three fingers and speckled with knobs of fat, but he doesn't really taste anything, eating it down, gulp, bite, gulp, bite. For a second, he sees a girl on the other side of the busy four-lane street who reminds him of Amelia, her platform shoes making her lurch and stop, as if she is trying to speed up and slow down at the same time. He wants to call out to her, even as he realizes she is not Amelia, fairer and much thinner, her bottom only imagined in her oversized jeans. He almost spits out his lunch to holler something, but he swallows again, breathes, watches her move past the dull eyes of empty stores until she turns the corner, swishing and lurching around a lamp post, and is gone.

After lunch, Harry heads back to the ice and the one o'clock Zamboni run. Because Mahmoud is watching, his thick, hairy forearms folded across his chest, Harry does the ice twice, the gloss so perfect it will take almost two hours for it to bunch up in frozen pebbles. He likes the feel of the water and brushes under him, the churning of the big machine making everything glint and shimmer like a mirage.

He is on the Zamboni, about to go over the last line of grainy ice, no giant eye this time, when he sees Amelia walk into the rink, rest against the skate counter, leaning hard on one elbow, her head in her hand. He is just about to call out to her, when he sees that something is different today, that her skin is as white as the ice, tucked in, almost, to her bones. Her body is different too, bent and angled, her hair straight and lanky down her back. For one second, he forgets he is on the Zamboni. He wants to jump off the machine, skid run across the ice in his workboots, and curl her into his body, take her home, put her in bed, read her stories. It's those dark circles under her eyes, he thinks, like when she used to get a fever or the flu.

But something keeps him on the hard black seat, something about Amelia's clothes, everything she is wearing looks gray and bunched and ominous, stained and wet, a blue striped flannel shirt tied around her waist. She's shivering, her arms bare, no jacket. She looks up toward the sound of the machine, but Harry sees she is not really looking at him. She squeezes her eyes shut, one slash of dark hair hugging her forehead.

Harry breathes in quick stabs of icy air, forgetting what he is doing, blood pulsing behind his eyes. All he wants to see is the ice, to feel the great machine under his body, to smooth the rink to a perfect, immaculate sheen, but it is no good now. Everything is water, just water, his eyes, Inez's vegetables steaming in aluminum vats, his daughter's clothes, the baby's open hand, so impossibly tiny.

The Possibility of Fire

"A don wa i," Robert says, his voice a soppy slur.

For the eighth time today, I wonder what it would be like to kill my ex-husband. The good news is that it would be easy. I wouldn't even have to touch his body. When I started to imagine killing him that was my first worry, blood on my hands and such.

"You have to eat it," I say instead of killing him. "It's part of your diet. You heard the nurse. Don't pretend your hearing's gone bad, too."

"Fuh yu," he says, turning away, scanning the dirty floor, his eyes connecting the bird shit yogurt splots.

Even though he can barely move, my ex-husband still has a temper.

I sit back in my chair, looking into the kitchen that used to be our kitchen but is now mine. After Robert left, I had it gutted and remodeled, installing stainless steel appliances and sleek granite. When it was done, I thought, this is a kitchen that will never bear witness to thrown plates and smashed glasses. This is a room that will never be a container for the word "fuck."

But I was wrong, though now "fuh" is the best Robert can do.

He looks at me, his right eye that old, mean eye, harsh and accusing. The left eye seems asleep, even though it is wide open, staring at me.

"Soo," he says. "No mo sht."

"I didn't make soup," I say, pushing the spoonful of organic vanilla yogurt through the cave door of his yellow teeth. "Tomorrow."

"Fuh yu." He swallows, smacks his lips, grins his horrible, lopsided grin. "Fuh yu."

I wouldn't have to plan too hard. All I would need to do is pour water down his throat. Every single visiting nurse warns me about aspiration.

"Slow and steady," they say. "Let him chew and swallow. Let him take in liquids one sip at a time. If anything goes into his lungs, it could mean pneumonia. And mostly, we don't catch it in these kinds of cases until it's progressed too far. So like I said. Slow and steady."

When Robert was my husband, he wrestled me—stumbling, lurching, gagging—over the open edge of the bedroom window, three stories up, threatened to let me fall. He threw a dictionary at my head, the hard leather edge whamming against my right cheekbone. He tripped me as I walked up the stairs. He slammed a car door on my hand. Robert has called me every known evil word in the two languages he knows. He did all these things in front of our sons, Tony and his older brother Sean. Sometimes before I fall asleep at night, I still hear them both crying and pleading, "Stop, Daddy. Stop."

Daddy only stopped when he was "fucking good and ready."

Later when Robert finally felt he needed to give us one, his big excuse was the drinking, which he eventually stopped, just before he left. Sean escaped to college, he left Tony and me in the hangover of his old habits and life, and went out to start over fresh. Rehab fixed him up for a new wife, who left him about a month after she found him shaking from stroke on the floor of their shiny new condo in San Francisco. Clutching her shopping bags, she discovered him long after aspirin would have been of any help. Other than the automatic monthly alimony payments (lawyer Robert thought this marriage was bullet-proof so there was no pre-nup), the last we heard from her were the final divorce papers.

And now I have him back, my ex-husband with two ex-wives.

"He has no one else," his sister Liz said the first time she called. In the background, I could hear her four children bouncing off the walls of her two-bedroom Florida panhandle condo. "After the hospitals and that woman, there's barely enough left for even a year in a convalescent facility."

"So let him stay there for a year," I said, my voice as hard as I could make it. "Then you can figure it out."

"What about Sean and Tony!" Liz said.

"He's your flesh and blood," I said. "Not mine."

"But Robert's your boys' father."

"Their father?" I said. "Do you know what their father was like?"

"Don't start with that. I mean, really. If it was so bad, why didn't you leave him? You had the chance. Tons of them."

I'd heard this before. From my mother when she was alive. From my sisters, too, both of whom stopped speaking to me after a while, unable to keep saying the same thing over and over again.

Liz sighed. "Look. I remember when you two fell in love. I know how crazy you were about him. And besides, no matter what, he is the father of your children."

I also remembered, skinny Liz in sandals and a halter dress standing shyly on the porch of the family home as Robert held my hand tight and introduced me, his new girlfriend. As Liz and their parents said hello and invited me into their home and family, I felt connected and whole. All because of Robert.

After that first phone call, I eventually hung up on Liz, but she was relentless, calling weekly, each time giving me some part of the past to hold up and examine: Robert arranging Sean and Tony on his shoulders so they could see the Fourth of July parade pass by, the family trip to Tahoe, Robert's and my wedding, Liz a geeky bridesmaid with shiny braces. During the fourth call, I kept thinking I would hang up like usual, but then I didn't. As I pressed the phone to my ear listening to Liz reel off the litany of Robert's woes, a space opened up for a different answer. I didn't know if I was afraid or excited. But something made me breathe faster.

"Fine," I said. "He can come home."

Now if I wanted to, I could wheel Robert over to the sliding glass door and topple him out onto the concrete steps, listening to his neck bones crack. On a cold rainy night, I could drive him in the wheelchair-accessible van and roll him to the middle of a forest or field and drive away. I could pour a pitcher of water down his throat and let him burble his way into a horrendous infection.

"Fuh yu," he says, knowing what I'm thinking, like he always did, even from across the room or on a different floor.

"Yeah," I say, spooning the last of the yogurt in his mouth. "We're done. I think I'm ready for a drink. Doesn't that sound good?"

Robert's right eye starts to cry.

"Maybe I'll make it a double, no rocks." I stand up and pick up the bowl. "It's such a shame you can't join me."

I stand over him, one hand on my hip, the hip Robert used to tell me was too big, too ugly, too fat. I was an "ugly fucking bitch whore" when he was drunk, and invisible when he was sober, not good enough to go with him to his law firm holiday parties, the annual partner celebrations, the firm's ball games and beach outings. He picked his second wife as though he were shopping at the new wife store, the slim, trim model for show *and* go, Sandy chesty, blond, and tan.

Robert looks at the table, mouthing his old favorite, ugly words, but he doesn't speak them, hoping that I might relent and give him what he wants. But that's never, ever going to happen.

At the support group, I sit next to Darl, whose wife Ann has multiple sclerosis. Apparently, this MS wasn't so bad when they were first married and even after the births of their two children, but now she's in her wheelchair all day long. Like me, Darl has visiting home healthcare nurses in and out of the house, a new one showing up without notice, all of them repeating instructions to him as though he were some kind of idiot.

"'Now, make sure you don't tire her out,'" Darl mimics, rubbing his forehead. "Like I'm taking her on marathons, for god's sake. We aren't even leaving the house! She can't even walk! Sometimes I wonder if she's even breathing!"

The group nods. Our therapist Sophie says something comforting in her low, modulated tone. But what can Sophie really tell him that will help anything? We all know this story. Darl, Gene, Ramona, Linh, Samantha, Brian, Todd, Trina, Jie, Pat. We know what's it's like for the health insurance not to pay for permanent care but to send out the flunkies who are just off the nursing school boat. What we need is a state-of-the art hospital, full-time nurses, attendants, cooks, housekeeping staff. We don't need anyone else to tell us what this is like. We know the odor of the evening kitchen, a fetid heap of plates and bowls smeared with food that can't even be called food anymore—glops of pureed mush, the stuff the nurses say helps "avoid aspiration."

We know the heft of a full bag of urine, the hot weight of paper towels full of shit. We know the mounds of sweaty, soiled laundry, when all of the above—kitchen, bathroom, bedroom—goes to hell, mess upon mess, nothing that any spot remover, mop, cleanser can fix. We know the sound of being alone in a house with "our" patients, their insistent, ragged breathing the only sound to interrupt a long twenty-four hours of nothing.

What Darl and I and the entire group need is a vacation in a five-star hotel, the kind that Robert took Sandy to on their month-long honeymoon through Italy. The type of ritzy establishment where you are helped out of a car, led up the steps, ushered into a foyer vast and grand, the air the exact perfect temperature, maybe 70 degrees. You are checked in by a SWAT team of workers, your bags rustled mysteriously through service elevators and side halls. When you walk into your suite, you are led through a magical mystery tour of cappuccino makers, free mini bar, hot tub, steam room, Turkish towels, premier bath and body products, and, most importantly, a view of ocean, snow covered mountain or cityscape of red-roofed villas from the platform of your plush, king-sized bed. At some point—maybe on your balcony where you sit with the one you love best and who loves you back the right way, both of you raising a glass of the complimentary champagne—you realize that you've forgotten every single part of your horrible life.

"Sorry about that," Darl says as we stack the community center's folding chairs. I pull his sweater from one, touch the insides of each pocket before handing it back. "I'm not on my game today."

"What game is that?" I ask, imagining a gruesome Sorry; an apt Trouble; a really bad, medical terminology Scrabble.

Darl gives me a dark, annoyed glance.

I shrug, sigh. "I'm not doing well myself."

"What about your younger son? Tony?" Darl asks. All of us know the names of loved ones and friends, the diminishing chain of relation, the people who now won't help as much as they used to or at all. "Isn't he pitching in?"

"He left for college," I say, feeling the pang under my left collarbone. "He didn't want to go."

"But you made him," Darl says. "Good mom. What about that older one?"

"Sean's still in New York."

Darl doesn't say anything, and I know he's thinking *ingrate, bad apple, pain-in-the-ass.*

Sean might be all these things, calling once a month as he does, not coming home for the holidays, refusing to let me put the phone to his father's ear when he does bother to call.

But I don't want him anywhere near here. I want him to stay

gone in a different version of his life. It took me a while to learn to hide Robert's bad moods, my bloody noses, black eyes, the head-to-foot numb feeling of fear. Sean saw all of it, heard the screams at night, followed my limp like a tracking dog, noticed me cradling my arm like a wounded animal. He watched me not leave over and over again. He saw his mother not protect herself his whole life. He deserves a lifetime reprieve.

Outside, it's almost dusk, the summer sky a lavender gray that clutches Lake Merritt. Darl and I head toward the sidewalk and our cars parked on Grand Avenue, but we don't stop like we should, getting back in our separate vehicles and heading home to face the nurse and her litany of terrible news: *didn't eat, won't talk, refused bath, yelled until I left the room.*

We wave to Samantha as she roars off in her yellow Mustang, but then we keep going, past the new restaurant and gas station and bookstore.

"If you could do anything differently, what would it be?" Darl asks.

I swallow, feeling a bad answer on my tongue. But instead, I say, "I wouldn't marry him."

Darl turns to me, and I flame red, knowing I sound bad, but that's only the top, tiny icy layer.

"Really?"

I nod.

"But then your kids," he says.

"I'd have different kids," I say, already mourning Sean and Tony as I let the sentence out into the air. The idea of their not-being fills me with nothing. But the reverse of this is true, too. They'd have different parents. All this story, gone.

"It was that bad," Darl says, surprising me.

I nod again, sodden with sadness, a watery, victimy goo that I have almost forgotten, the slurpy mess I floated in for years.

"Maybe I wouldn't have married Ann," he says. "But I probably would, even knowing. I loved her so much. Things looked like they might turn out just fine."

"They always do," I say, remembering the way Robert turned to me so often those first two years, his eyes sparkly with hope and joy and love. What I did was right. Who I was, was right, too. "And then they don't."

Darl doesn't say anything for a while. We cross the street, heading over to the Grand Lake Theatre that flashes bright into the growing darkness, the titles of all the movies dark like blackened teeth against the glowing white sign.

"I haven't seen a movie in a long time," he says, staring up at the list, reminding me of my boys and those Sundays I would take them to a movie, their choice. We'd go when Robert was out at a bar, using our moments of freedom wisely. The boys would pick adventure, sci-fi, animation, and I would sit still in the mystery of peace, all my attention on movies I would never pick for myself. The story would take me over, and I would relax into lives so not mine. But the anxiety would creep back as the credits rolled, and I had to take us back home.

"Do you want to go?" I ask, the words out before I can pull them back, more on their tail. "Maybe there's one that starts now."

For a moment, I see Darl's hope. He looks at me, brown eyes wide, a smile on his face, the idea that something so spontaneous and remarkable could happen. A thrill, just as it is for me. For maybe two hours, for just a little while, we could be gone.

As Darl considers, I can see him as a younger man, the man who decided not to marry Ann, who moved on to the next woman or the next after that. A man who wouldn't be standing on this busy street corner with a woman like me.

"Well," he says, looking up at the list and the posted times next to the title.

Even I do the math. I search for a 7:20, 7:30, and nothing until 8:10. Inside me, something inflated pops.

"I—" he begins.

"I know," I say. "Me, too."

Finally, it's quiet. The nurse and I wrangled Robert into bed, and she gave me that look, the one that signals *I'm not coming back to this hell fuck shit hole ever again.*

Trust me, I've seen it before.

Robert thrashed and swung his good arm. He yelled and swore his awkward swears, but then he finally allowed us to bathe him and put him to bed. The way he falls asleep now reminds me of when he used to drink, the sudden, deep crash into silent, immobile unconsciousness.

"I saw some of your food in the fridge," the nurse said before she left. "It's too chunky. I showed you how to puree. You need to worry about him aspirating that."

I turned to her and saw that she was giving me her last piece of good advice.

"Thanks," I said, closing the front door behind her.

Now my hands are deep into soapy water, and I'm washing all the dishes from the entire day, from breakfast to dinner and in between. Outside, I hear nothing, no cars, no whine of streetlight, no crickets, though it must be cricket time. Once, back when Sean was a baby, back in the time before it all started, a cricket somewhere in our backyard stayed alive for months, sawing away all through December. It was the early winter after the Oakland Hills fire, our house just on the edge of the evacuation zone. On a bad day, we could still smell char, and the drive down Highway 13 and up onto 24 was like passing through a smoldering war zone.

Maybe something happened to cricket eggs or crickets in the conflagration, but this hardy cricket was the lone survivor, a fire cricket, a sad summer guitar amidst the Christmas carols.

Now I pause, wait, and nothing. Not even a crazed, fuzzy moth batting up against the screen door.

I pull up the plug and the water swirls down the drain. I wipe down the counters, the dining room table, and sweep all the floors. Just as I'm putting away the broom, my phone rings with Tony's special ring, and my heart does a wild beating thing against my ribs, a one-two, pound-pound.

I want to cry. My sweet Tony, wanting to stay at home instead of going to college. My sweet, sweet boy who said, "Mom, I'll go. But you come with me. Just please come with me."

I don't answer the phone. I can't.

Outside, as I sit on the curb across from the house, I remember the day of the fire. We'd spent the afternoon on College Avenue, strolling past the restaurants and popping into the stores, Sean bundled up against a wind that I realized wasn't cold but warm, pushed over Mt. Diablo, whooshing all the way past San Francisco, an off-shore flow.

Robert seemed upset that day, angry, and later, I would recognize his behavior as the beginning of the cycle, the signal that my life was going to get a lot worse before it got better. But that October day, I could still imagine that he was irritated because of work or from living with a baby who cried all night long.

"What the hell is that smell?" he said as we drove up Pleasant Valley Road and then turned left on Moraga. "It's like a campfire, only worse."

For some reason, I'd been scared to answer, fearing that my first thought—fire—would be wrong. Stupid, even. So I turned to him, smiled, shrugged, but he wasn't paying attention to me for once, barreling up the hill and pulling over on the side of the road, both of us getting out of the car. Other people were standing by their cars, pointing up at the Montclair Hills, and there it was. The whirring lick of fire, the pulse of smoke, white and gray and then swirling black. All around us were the sounds of sirens. Overhead, helicopters whapped.

"Holy shit," he said. "The whole world's on fire."

I stepped closer to him, and he reached out for me, pulling me close. His hand was tight around my waist, his grip hard, as if he were worried, scared that I might be lost to the flames. In that instant, I was needed, loved, the way I'd always hoped for.

"We've got to get home," he said. "We might have to evacuate."

And then he pulled me even closer and kissed me, the way he used to before I got pregnant and fat and dull, the way he did all those years ago on his parents' porch steps.

"Let's go," he said, putting me in the car and checking on Sean who was finally fast asleep. "I've got to get you both to safety."

We drove home, right here, to this same house and watched the news for the rest of the day, long into the night, waiting for the call to flee. As Robert stared red-eyed at the TV screen, I padded softly into Sean's room to pack his diaper bag, putting in all we'd need for at least a week: tiny t-shirts, wipes, pants with snaps. But then the winds shifted, and I was so relieved because everything was going to be all right.

Now I stare at the dark house that survived the fire. I reach my hand into my pocket and feel for the lighter, the one I took from Darl's sweater pocket, wrapping my hand around its slick plastic shape. I pull it out, rubbing the tiny metal wheel with my thumb. I flick it once, twice, watch the sparks. I flick it again, watch it burn.

That Strip of Earth

He is running on the beach, the waves a slow false slap on the shoreline. He wants to get home, and that's why he's running. Why he's running and not driving is because he's drunk. Why he's drunk is because of what happened at the party—before he started drinking and then afterward. But he's a smart boy—he's been told this by everyone—and doesn't want to lose anything: his car and his college fund. He doesn't want his mother's gaze to shift. Even as he runs, he can see her face, the way she turns to look at him when he comes in the door. Her eyes wide, waiting, relieved that it is he who has come home. She pats the couch, she moves over, collecting her newspaper and crossword puzzles, pencils, and reading glasses. He plops down, able to tell her almost everything about his day. Things are good. Things are going to be fine, now and later and forever.

He's held it together, so no, nothing will change. Not now. Not for this thing that no one can know about, so he runs, his shirt unbuttoned, his jeans wet, unbelted, stained on the knees in dark circles.

Even with only starlight, he can see the dock and then knows to look right for the rowboat and the canoe and the path that will lead to the lane and then his street. He will be there in what? Seven minutes? He will sneak around the back of the house, up the wisteria vine—decades old, thick and knotty—and crawl in his window. His mother will never have to know.

Betty couldn't help herself, actually. It was because the woman Jill—a girl, sort of, even though she must be in her late forties—was a stranger. But nice. A teacher. Kind and likely caring. She has large breasts and a rounded stomach, the kind of woman who breastfed her babies for too long and took solid afternoon naps on a well-worn couch. The kind of woman who ate chocolate without worrying.

Jill would listen. She would be interested. Also, Betty would never see her again after this odd forced tour week together, the eighteen of them on a bus wending through the Irish hills. A famous castle. A famous stone. A famous crystal factory. A famous church.

And then every night here as with every night for fifty-five years, Betty would lie down to sleep with Art. She on her back, he snoring, her thoughts a darkness over them, her constant, unwavering loss and ache heavier than any hotel duvet. He doesn't wake to comfort her or tell her a story. He doesn't talk of things other than golf or grandchildren or the damn economy. At least, he hasn't for years, thinking along with everyone else that she should be over it. That her grief is done.

Betty's feet hurt, both Achilles tendons stretched like taffy after too many power walks and tennis games, not to mention today's hike around the castle grounds. Art was up in the room taking a nap. Jill's over-chatty mother was off buying a hat or some Chapstick in the hotel store. "Chapped lips! I'm still so thirsty after all those hours in the airplane," she'd said before toddling off. She was probably Betty's age but acted older.

As they relaxed on the large bar couch, Jill looked at Betty and tried not to roll her eyes. Betty gave her a conspiratorial grin, an "Oh, how do you put up with her?" But the smile stilled and almost cracked. Her own daughter Lily was too busy with her three children and husband to come to dinner on Sunday, much less travel across the world with Betty to see things neither of them cared about. She would like to sit here with Lily, warm and cozy and tired, and have Lily take her hand.

"Mother," this imagined Lily would say. "Tell me about that night. Tell me everything about my brother."

"It's a miracle we haven't killed each other." Jill sipped her gin-and-tonic. But Betty had seen Jill reach out for her mother's hand, hold it as the tour group walked like school children in rows up cobblestone streets. They sat together on the bus and talked about the passing landscapes and vistas. At dinner time, they exclaimed over the seafood chowder and light-as-air desserts.

"You travel together often?" Betty asked, wondering what it would be like to go anywhere with an adult child. When her children were little, they clung to her legs and hands. They reached up for her when she leaned over their cribs and then beds.

When had the affection become a turned-cheek kiss?

Jill nodded, her chin comfortable on her neck, her neck on her chest, her chest slipping onto the mound of her stomach. "Her brother—my uncle—died. They used to go somewhere big every summer. Giving up her travel seemed like a last step she wasn't ready for. So off we went."

Betty felt her mouth open, but she could tell her response would turn into a sound not language. So she swallowed, thought about when moving forward stopped everything, lingering on the verb *to step*.

"That's nice." She looked out the window onto the parking circle, rain-slicked and gleaming. "Lovely."

"Do you have children?"

Betty watched the cars, windshield wipers throwing arcs of water everywhere.

"Yes," she said, turning back to Jill, her story changing. How her mouth felt, her jaws as tight as the old castle door. "Two. A boy and a girl."

Jill turned to look at her, and Betty felt the words slip past. "But my son died."

Just before he reaches the dock, he yanks to a stop. He breathes hard, but catches his breath after a shocked one-two inhale. He runs every day, and it is only how far from the Abbotts' house? Two miles? But his heart pounds in places it shouldn't, the thrum in his fingertips and ankles and shoulders. He can feel his skin in all these unusual places. For the first time in his life, he feels the knobs of his spine. A press, an *ah*, a press, an *ah*, all the way down to his sacrum. He wants to touch exactly there and there and there, but instead, he puts his hands on his hips and turns to watch the lake, a pool of clear nothing.

He wants to go back to the forest, the dark, the hands, the mouths, both their bodies. He wants to go home.

Looking down at his feet, only the moons of his toenails visible—he so tan already—he knows he could go back to the party. Everything could return to the second he'd jerked away from Matthew and his warm, wet mouth. His fear and desire working to keep him still. He pushed back, pulled closer, then ran, backward, and then forward, pulling on his clothes as he moved through the trees and shrubs.

An owl hoots. Across the water, someone slams a door, the echo skimming toward him.

He walks forward and then stops again, slamming down on his knees. He cups his face in his hands and cries the way he must have as a child, the sobs dragged out hard and silent from the bottom of his lungs. The time he lost his toy train. The day he missed the bus and his mother wasn't home to pick him up. When he didn't make the junior high track team. When his father refused to get him a dog.

He's so tired, so exhausted. He wants to stay here where it's dark and quiet. Where he's alone.

"Just stay the course," his high school counselor said at their last meeting. "You're a shoo-in at Harvard."

"You could apply closer to home!" his mother said, when she saw all the college catalogues. "For heaven's sake!"

"It's yours to lose," his father said. "One bad step and. . ." He snapped his fingers, the sound a whip.

"Don't leave," Matthew whispered moments ago in the woods. "Please, please, please don't leave."

He wants to leave. He wants to stay, but only for short pieces of time he can escape from. Here, gone. Here, gone.

Here, Matthew's hands on his chest, sliding up to his neck, pulling his face to his. A kiss, their first kiss last year. His first kiss. His second kiss, his fiftieth kiss, and with Matthew, the kid from first grade who grew up to be six-foot, one sixty-five, long blond hair to his shoulders. A swimmer. A pool outside and inside, a calm clear body of water in Matthew's gaze. An open expanse of yes. Matthew, who knew who he was. Matthew, who tonight did what they'd both wanted. Tonight, he'd let go of everything. School. His girlfriend Annie. His father's rules. Matthew pulled him outside, and yes. Yes. He allowed it, tired of staying the course. Wanting to stay close to home. Wanting Matthew more than anything else.

Hands, mouth, the tree holding him up, Matthew kissing and touching and moving down his body. His hands on Matthew's soft hair, holding him tight against his body. But always, his focus couldn't stay with lips and hands and tongues. He'd flinched at the crackle of branch, the flicker of white. Annie, looking for him, her thin arm on a tree limb. Annie's pale face in the flashlight, wide open with the truth of their entire high school relationship.

"We should wait," he'd told her every Friday night as they rolled around on her living room rug, the back of his mother's station wagon, the deep mats in the high school gym. "I don't want to ruin things."

Annie would sigh, roll onto her back, both of them holding onto the script he was writing for them, one that everyone could understand. Good student. Good athlete. Nice girlfriend. Off to great college. He'd thought he could hang on until he left. Somehow, he'd bring Matthew with him. Somehow, it would work out. But later, away from here and the explanations he'd have to provide, the lies or truths he'd have to tell.

But things were ruined in her muffled yelp, the rush of her quick steps in the woods, Matthew's hands trying to hold him still, Matthew unaware that they'd been seen at last.

"Please, don't! Please."

Then he ran.

"I'm so sorry," Jill said. "Oh, my! That's terrible."

She was polite, this girl. Betty had heard it all, the questions before, the "When did it happen?" and the "Oh, it was so long ago. That must give you some comfort."

But everyone who said so was wrong. It was not long ago. It was just yesterday. It was now. It could be tomorrow, she still desperate to drive to the party and pick up Stephen, drag him to the car, press him into to the passenger's seat, and zoom home. Or better, take him to another county, state, country. Planet. Take him away from whatever it was that made him run away from the party and head through the woods. That's what dear sweet Annie later told her. Annie who always believed in Stephen. Went to every track meet. Showed up to family dinners wearing a proper dress, her hair straight and perfect and falling to her shoulders.

"He was there, and then he wasn't," Annie had said that night, her face wet, eyes red and puffy and stunned, her hair blown back, her whole body shaking. "I saw him run into the forest."

It had been so dark that night. Betty hadn't seen a thing when she glanced outside the window before bed, though she'd imagined she could see the party. Behind her, Art snored.

"Something you can never get over," Jill said. "I'm so sorry."

Betty was ready to nod as she usually did. She felt her head move up, but then there were tears, hard and solid in her mouth and throat. Stephen beating in her chest. How she could see him running. How she could reach out and hold up her hand, yell, "Stop! Don't move a muscle!"

But then and now, Jill's hand on her shoulder, Betty couldn't say a word. All she was able to do was sink into the end of the story, the terrible way it closed each and every time she ran through it.

He was there, and then he wasn't.

A bat twirls overhead, a rustle in the dark sky. Stephen follows the swirl with his eyes, the bat skittering up and then rushing out over the water. Behind him, he can still hear the whine of the party music. Matthew is back there somewhere. Outside still. Or maybe inside, trying to act natural, whatever that means. Not having seen Annie, Matthew must think Stephen ran off because of mouth and tongue.

Stephen turns to his right. There's his house, the kitchen light on, as it always is when he's out. His parents upstairs, his father dead asleep. Some nights, his mother leaves him a sandwich. Others, a plate of cookies. Normal. His mother held out an ordinary happy life as if it were a plate of cookies. How much easier to accept than to decline. How much easier to just go home. He reaches out his hand. He can pretend home is that close.

But he's left home already. He knows that, even if no one else does. He left home the moment he had this secret. His longing for Matthew. Really, his not-longing for Annie. For any girl. With Matthew's first kiss, Stephen cracked off the family shelf like an iceberg.

Wind whisks his neck. Stephen walks toward the water, turning back toward the music, pausing in the sound. He knows that once floating free, ice has only to melt before it becomes the ocean.

He glances home one more time. For a second, he imagines he sees his mother's flickering form in her dark window. Stephen lifts a hand and waves. He wants her to know he understands. But she has to see him, too. Stephen closes his eyes and breathes in Matthew, feels his hands on his shoulders, tastes his skin.

It's who I am, he thinks. It's what I want.

Stephen turns back to go find Matthew. He walks fast; he swings his arms. He runs.

Instrumental music filled the bar. A flute. A violin. Betty ordered another Jameson. Jill put down her drink on the shiny wooden table.

"When?" she began and then changing course. "How?"

Betty reached for her new drink. There they are again, those old lady hands, brown-spotted from years of tennis, golf, and sunbathing, though now—too late—she wears sunscreen. Her joints thickened with arthritis, her left index finger pulled in, that hand almost a triangle.

"He'd be fifty-two now," Betty said. "Maybe a grandfather himself."

Jill waited, her smooth fingers around her glass.

"It was right after the summer of his junior year. Sixteen. Almost seventeen. He'd almost gotten through high school perfectly. All A's. Track team. He could run like the wind. He was so lovely to watch. Like some kind of African animal. You know, all that golden grass and a sleek body of muscle zipping through like a blade."

In the lobby, Jill's mother talked to the concierge, the up and down of annoying questions. A loud laugh. More questions.

"That night, he went to a party with his girlfriend Annie. They were so cute together. They were so young. It would have been almost impossible for them to have married, but I always hoped they might." Sometimes before falling asleep, Betty had imagined Stephen and Annie at twenty-eight, coming home to visit with their two waif-like children, both with Stephen's dark eyes. Once she'd joked with Stephen about it but only once. That look on his face. "But they'd had a fight. Right in the middle of the party. He ran off. Into the woods and toward the shore of the lake we lived on back then. If he'd kept going, nothing would have happened. But for some reason, he stopped."

Betty stopped, looked up at Jill who met her gaze. "Did he stop somewhere important?"

"They found the place. He'd walked around a bit. In a circle. Must have been staring at the water. Thinking about Annie. How to make up with her. They'd been going out for three years."

"Did you ever go to the spot?" Jill asked.

Inside, Betty shuddered, all her organs vibrating with *no*, recoil, horror. She had never again stepped on that strip of earth. She couldn't bear to share his last horrible moments with sand or soil. She didn't need to see where he died because she could still feel it.

"Maybe it was too hard," Jill said, her voice soft.

Betty doesn't stop to answer. "So like I said, he stopped. And then instead of walking back up to the woods toward home, he started running along the water's edge, headed back to the party."

She felt the worst part of the story rise up and press against her breastbone. This was the part that people were listening for. This was the part she could never speak of to people she had to see again. If she did, if she had, Betty would forever be marked by her sorrow on the outside, the way she was in her heart. But this woman would go away, and maybe she could take part of the ache with her.

"You don't—" Jill said.

"He was running. He was running, and he didn't know about the workers. The live electrical cable."

"Live?" Jill asked. "How did that happen?"

"Everyone blamed someone else. The neighborhood hadn't been notified. The gas and electric workers made a mistake, you see. Left the cable down right there on the beach. Didn't cut off the power. It was dark, and he was running to get back to Annie, and he stepped right on it. His best friend found his body thirty feet from the wire."

The pounding on the door. Betty's hand at her throat. How long it seemed for Art to wake up. Flicking on the porch light, she'd opened the door to find Matthew, his body covered in dirt and sand, his hands dangling at his sides, his face stricken. The calls. The sirens. Matthew waiting in the kitchen for the police and fire-fighters. Annie showing up and sitting motionless at the table. All night, they both stayed in the kitchen with her and Art and listened to the men talk about what happened. Annie still sent Christmas cards. Where had Mathew gone to? Why had he disappeared from their lives? But both of them must have a cache of stories Betty had never heard, stories about Stephen's hopes and dreams and desires.

"Stephen would be 52," Betty said, even though she knew she'd already said that. "A grown man. A man heading into the last half of his life."

Jill began to talk, almost humming the words, a comfort, a lullaby. But no words would ever comfort Betty. She knew that then, and she knew it still. Nothing helped. Not her daughter's life: Lily's successes and bright children. Not charity work. Not money. Not alcohol or time or her husband. Not travel. Not Ireland or Russia or Sicily.

Nothing could ever bring her back to that evening. Nothing could allow her to reach out to Stephen's arm and say, "Stay home tonight. I want to talk with you. Sit down. Sit here by me. Grab that blanket. Tell me about your dreams, my dear, dear son. My lovely boy. Tell me everything. All of it."

Betty made some additional comments and then gently turned the talk to other, lesser losses. By the time the conversation was over, they were relating the differences between first- and business-class seats. Finally, Jill's mother wandered in with her tiny shopping bag. Jill stood, pressed Betty's shoulder one more time, and then took her mother's arm. The two of them excused themselves and clambered up the main staircase. Betty knew she should wake up Art for dinner. But instead, she ordered another drink.

Once, long before he'd retired, Art came home from the office, his eyes red. Betty watched him as he stood in front of the family room window, staring out at the water.

Finally, he said, "I can't drive down the road without thinking about him. I drive all the way around the lake to not see where it happened."

Alone, Betty sat on the couch, staring at the Irish amber clinging to her glass. In a few years or maybe even months, she'd be dead. But she would feel this loss even then. Her body might stop and then rot in her own box, but there would be no release.

All those years ago, Art had turned to her, his face wet. "I see him running, Betty. He's running. He's still running. I can never get to him. I hold out my arms, and I never make it. Not ever. Not once."

Accepted Forms of Ruin

"I don't want to be a bother," Julia's mother said on the phone, the call coming in after Julia had eaten half a box of crackers and most of a pot of soft, spreadable cheese flecked with chives. Now in front of her, her boss's open emails, all of which required responses. Julia worked in banking, assistant to Deb, a wealth-management executive, who was only sporadically in the office and whose work Julia did at one-twentieth the pay. Maybe less. She was never asked to, but she put in more hours than were in her job description, arriving at the Palo Alto office at 6:45 am and leaving for home at 7 pm to go eat Thai take-out or crackers, the television on but muted. After eating over her sink and then opening her junk mail, she would sit at her computer until 11 pm answering emails.

"Mom." Julia hadn't talked to her mother in two weeks or visited her since the holidays, so she forced herself to turn away from the computer. "You're not a bother. What's wrong?"

"I went to the doctor last week. Things have been…Listen, it's all about my stomach. I had a few tests."

In that instant, Julia knew it was her fault. Because of her, her mother's systems were shutting down. After all these years, the thing rotting inside Julia had finally spread into her mother. Connie should have been safe when Julia was in college across the country; later, after she graduated, she'd hoped the two hundred miles between the Bay Area and Chico would be enough. Now it was clear Julia should have just stayed home and gone to Chico State to save money, helping her mother out with the house. The distance and separation hadn't been far enough; her mother had caught it anyway.

"What do you have?"

"Maybe, well. Maybe it's cancer. It's not—"

Julia stopped breathing, her mouth open, her eyes wide and staring at the glowing computer screen and the list of emails.

Send follow up to Glen about portfolio.

Four chocolate, two vanilla. Staff meeting.

Portia needs pickup 4:30 p.m.

Quarterlies!

She blinked.

"What?" she began.

"Now, honey. Don't cry. Listen, if it is what they think, I'm going to have surgery next week. I—okay. Stop. It's going to be fine. I know you don't like to be here, but I hope you can drive up for a day."

But Julia was already typing her email to Deb, asking for two of the ten weeks of vacation she had never taken. Though she was pretty sure Deb wouldn't say no, if she did, Julia would quit. She'd quit things before. Therapy, three times. People, too. In fact, she was good at it.

"Mom," Julia said. "I'll be there tomorrow."

It had been raining since September. Now, in mid-February, the Central Valley was a marshy slog, roads, levees, and dams barely keeping the water from forming a great lake from Redding to Bakersfield. Lake Oroville was an official disaster, the broken spillway forcing evacuations from several nearby towns. Entire populations were huddled in gymnasiums and Red Cross centers as engineers monitored the spillway and forecasters followed weather forming in the Pacific.

"Has it ever rained this much?" Julia said last week as she looked out at the billowing gray clouds, the constant view from their fifth-floor office. It had been summer for a very long time and then not. She'd lived in California most of her life, but this rainy season seemed like the apocalypse.

"Back in the day," Julia's coworker Arturo had said without looking up. He sat at the desk in front of hers, his computer screen open to constant, winding pages of code he wrote in a computer language called Python. Julia wasn't sure what he did, exactly, but it involved all the division's data. Plus, he liked to talk about virtual reality.

"It's so much better than real life," he always said.

Arturo was a sixth-generation Californian, fluent in stuff Julia never thought about, like historical rainfall totals and the destruction of native populations.

"When will it stop?" Julia had asked.

Arturo turned around, flattening the spring of dark hair that shot upward from his scalp, no matter the amount of product. His wedge of hair was even more surprising because he shaved the sides and back. Sometimes, his head and neck resembled a perfect circle of sod cut free of a lawn and tossed on a lamppost.

And because of his odd mop, he reminded her of a puppet, a good one, a crazy furry creature from a children's TV show. The kind that might seem strange but was nicer than expected. Arturo's eyes were shining black disks that always took her in. When he handed her reports or cups of coffee, she noted his hands were soft. He was the only man she'd been comfortable being nearby since high school.

With a whir of motion, he flicked his mouse, a rain gauge popping up on his computer screen. "It's only February. Thirty-eight inches and counting. Back before dams, the Sierra snowpack melted and formed a huge lake. You could take a boat from Rio Vista to Roseville."

"What were we thinking?"

"Same old," Arturo said. "We ruined everything. We built dams so we could water ski and plant kiwi fruit and watermelon in the desert. But Mother Nature is fighting back. Oroville and environs are doomed."

So to avoid the swelling lake in the middle of the state, Julia took a different route home. Julia held the steering wheel at ten and two, trying to slide down to three and nine, which had been determined the safest position. She kept her eyes riveted on the road, braking slowly on the rain-slick streets, spotting crosswalks and errant pedestrians. Instead of driving up Highway 99 through Yuba City, Palermo, and Oroville, Julia stayed on 5, turning off onto 45 after Arbuckle.

"Take my car," Deb had said when Julia checked in at the office. "Seriously."

"I can't do that," Julia said, unable to look at the keys, focusing on Deb's French-manicured nails, silver bracelet, tanned fingers.

"I mean it!" Deb put the Mercedes keys in her palm. "Besides, you know I'll be in Seattle. We'll figure it out if you need it for longer."

The weather was so bad, Julia was relieved that she wasn't rattling around in her used Accord, one taillight sketchy, the back brakes worn to slim wafers.

The thick windshield wipers whooshed back and forth, back and forth, as the rain spattered and slapped the windows. Wind buffeted the car. Julia clung on tight as she passed by sloshy rice fields and farmhouses, leaning a little forward, focusing on the road that glowed a speckled yellow in the headlights. She ignored her phone ringing in her purse. The *ding ding* of messages.

Deb and Deb. Maybe Arturo. Deb.

Her mother refused to text, so at least Julia didn't have to worry about that.

Up front, Julia imagined the figure in the seat next to her. Hunched over, the figure ignored her and looked out the window, face averted, her head covered in a hoodie but one made of anger and blame.

"I'm sorry," Julia began the way she always did. "I didn't know."

The figure said nothing, as usual. But she turned to face Julia, waiting for the very thing Julia couldn't give her. Her face was pale, still beautiful, but vague. Like the idea of a face. Like memory. Like smoke.

"You never listen," Julia said.

A pickup truck roared past, spraying water. Julia slowed, though the Mercedes' tires felt glued to the wet road. Hydroplaning occurred at speeds higher than thirty-five, and it was worse in the wind. But there was also low visibility, fog, and general reduced traction to consider. Behind her, someone flashed his lights off and on, so she sped up to almost fifty, feeling the velocity in her jaw.

"I had a runny nose," she said. "I was so embarrassed. Mrs. Franklin said we couldn't line up for recess because someone had stolen Laura's pens. We had to wait until the person raised a hand, remember?"

The figure in the seat stayed silent.

"I had a runny nose and had to pee, and all I asked you for was a Kleenex. You had those nice ones in the packet in your desk."

As she drove, Julia felt her six-year-old body clench, desperate to hold in her bodily fluids, urine and mucous and tears. Knees pressed together, nose streaming, eyes full, she willed Mrs. Franklin to sigh and let them go play.

"You ignored me," Julia said.

The figure turned away and bent into a knot of invisibility.

Before the worst happened that day in class, the boy who sat next to her, Michael Schutz, saw Julia's streaming nose and started to laugh, snorting at his desk. He was compact, smart, blue-eyed; he knew math and art, his drawn Australia the best, his clay platypus on display. He was the fastest of all the boys, his curly hair bouncing as he ran.

"Little snotty nerd face," he whispered, laughing with Marie-Therese who sat in front of Julia.

Mrs. Franklin strode in front of the class, her hands behind her back. "Everyone, arms on your desk, heads down. I'll do it as well. Whoever stole the pens just needs to come up here and put them on my desk. No questions asked. All our eyes will be shut tight. One, two, three, now."

Julia loved the sound of the scratchy felt on thick pieces of construction paper. On her way into class, she'd slipped a careful hand into Laura's desk, and right now, they were in her own, tucked under her binder. But she had to pee so bad, she couldn't walk up to the front of the room to return them even if she wanted to. She'd wiped snot on both hands, her face red.

"Please," she whispered before they all put their heads down.

"No," Marie-Therese said looked straight at Julia, her voice flat and calm. She was so fair, Julia could see a thin blue vein pulsing at her temple when she smiled at Michael.

"Please," Julia whispered, but she felt her will stretch as thin as a Kleenex.

Both Marie-Therese and Michael giggled, heads ducked down to avoid Mrs. Franklin's gaze.

It was slow at first, but then exactly the way she would have on the toilet at home. A gush, and then the reek of urine.

"Mrs. Franklin! Julia's peeing all over the floor!" Michael called out.

"Oh, my God!" Marie-Therese jumped up and scurried away

from the puddle pooling under Julia's desk. "You're disgusting!"

Her hair swayed around her body, her eyes wide, her slim hands reaching out to the other girls who swarmed around her.

"Children!" Mrs. Franklin called, but then the boys started a circling, a stampeding, a raucous calling out of names and wild hilarity. Someone pushed open the classroom door, and everyone spilled out onto the playground shrieking.

Mrs. Franklin walked over to Julia, two towels in her hands.

"Oh, dear," she said. "Let me…start to clean up."

"I stole the pens," Julia sobbed.

"Of course you did," Mrs. Franklin said. "Stay here. I'll get some soap and water. And I'll get the office to call your mother."

And then Julia was alone in the classroom, pee puddling in her shoes.

She stole the pens, and she peed herself. Of course.

"All you had to do was give me the Kleenex," Julia said now, her voice a slim whine against the pounding rain. The figure shimmered and began to fold into thin air. "I could have made it. I would have been okay."

But both Julia and the figure next to her knew she was wrong.

She reached her mother's house before noon, walking up to the front porch as she searched for her key, the same one her mother had given her in third grade, the year her father finally left for good and Connie had to go back to work at the library.

"It's just you and me now. You have a big responsibility," Connie had said, handing Julia the key on a leather keychain. "You have the keys to our only castle."

The three-bedroom, two-bath castle seemed smaller now, shabbier, the door needing a coat of paint, the windows smudged from dogs' noses. Even the doormat seemed small, a shoddy, hardly welcoming rectangle. The rain had stopped, but the two huge California walnut trees in the front yard were sodden, the trunks slick and black, the branches bare but with the beginning of leaf buds. The lawn was the same lush swath of green from Julia's childhood, thick Bermuda grass that withstood drought and the blazing Chico summer sun.

In the shrubberies, the whistles of blackbirds. Overhead, three crows swooping down and into the hedgerows, cawing. When Julia closed the front door, her mother appeared in the front hall, a dish towel in her hands. Her two golden retrievers Belle and Butch spun tawny circles around Julia and snuffled her hands.

"There you are! I've been trying to call you all morning! I was about to call the police."

Julia dug in her purse and looked at her phone. Every single message was from her mother. Even one rare text. Deb and Arturo had texted but only to ask if her mother was okay.

She slid the phone back in her purse and hugged her mother, breathing in the smells of dish soap and coffee grounds. She allowed herself to relax, breathe in once, and then she stepped back before she started to cry.

"What's wrong?" Julia stared into her mother's eyes.

Her mother put her hands on Julia's shoulders, reaching up as she did. Julia had grown past her during high school, but now it seemed her mother had shrunk, slipped into her clothes and shoes, closer to the ground.

"Nothing's wrong!" Connie said. "It's good news. I don't have cancer at all. It's an ulcer."

"What?"

"I know," Connie said, leading Julia into the house. The dogs followed along, their collars jangling. "And now I'm on an antibiotic and an antacid before bed. One dose this morning, and I'm already feeling better."

"Just like that?"

"I'm sorry, honey. I shouldn't have dragged you into this. But they did one last scan yesterday and called this morning with the results."

Julia felt air and hope return to her body. She reached out for her mother's hand, squeezing. "Mom, that's great."

"I agree. So in celebration, I made a lasagna. Let me take it out of the oven. It needs to rest a bit."

Julia knew the intimate details of her mother's sort-of home-made lasagna (homemade unless you counted store-bought noodles and jarred sauce). It was a featured casserole in Julia's childhood, the big pan her mother made on Friday and that they ate off of for days. With a salad. Cold. Reheated with garlic bread. Cold. Then on to lentil soup, mac and cheese, spaghetti with meatballs, ham with pineapple rings, roast chicken with pan-fried potatoes. Repeat.

No wonder her mother had an ulcer. Connie pulled open the oven and took out a lasagna, the room steaming and spicy with tomato and meat.

"I'm going to the bathroom. Clean up."

"Take your time. This thing is still bubbling like witches' brew."

Julia headed out of the warm kitchen and into the hall. Outside, the sky was grey, nothing but a gloomy glow of white coming through the skylight. The bedroom doors closed, the hallway was dark, a passage in a submerged submarine. Each carpeted step brought her back, dragged her down. How many times had she made this journey from kitchen to bathroom, kitchen to her bedroom, kitchen to her mother's bedroom where she could curl up and finally sleep? Sure, she'd survived the peeing incident, and it helped that in third-grade, Chico Unified School District opened up another elementary school and half the kids in her second-grade class were transferred.

The day she learned Marie-Therese was one of the students transferring felt like a holiday. Marie-Therese could have the shiny buildings and computers; Michael Schutz and all the other girls who still teased Julia, calling out, "Does anyone smell pee?" or "Who's wearing yellow?"

Julia didn't see the worst of them again until high school, and by then, they were mostly too polite to mention that terrible day in class. As for Marie-Therese, she spun around in her desk when Julia walked into social studies the first day of freshman year. She smiled a little, her eyes cold. Julia flushed, blurting out, "Hi" much too loudly, but Marie-Therese flicked her long, thick hair and turned back to her friend, a girl Julia didn't recognize, someone who didn't know the story, at least not yet.

Michael Schutz's family had moved away, and by the start of 10th grade, Julia was able to let go of the clenched feeling in her trembling thighs, the horror of the smell wafting up from the wet floor, Mrs. Franklin's urgent but kind voice. The inevitable returning of the pens to Laura. Then her mother's murmuring that went on for years. "It was nothing. It happens to everyone."

That was a lie. It never happened to anyone else. But it didn't matter except in a dark corner of Julia's heart. She wasn't popular, but she'd made friends, girls she called at night and texted during class. She was invited to birthday parties and overnights. Boys smiled at her as she walked down the halls. At the end of junior year, Matthew Denny asked her to meet him at a party, and from then on, they'd been a thing. Together. As Julia headed into her senior year, the terrible peeing incident was worn down to a whisper, a ghost, except for that cold look in Marie-Therese's eyes, the same look that said, "You are not good enough for a tissue."

Marie-Therese never said anything about it, nothing mean or nice. She never paid attention to Julia because Marie—as she was now called—was popular and beautiful, quiet and self-assured.

Julia saw Marie's confidence in the way she held her books, the smooth swirl of her hips as she walked, the way she flicked her hair over her shoulders, a habit she never lost. She wore little makeup and clothes that were almost conservative, but under her sweaters and scarves and almost European wraps, t-shirts, and jeans was a body Julia could only imagine having: long legs, small waist, big but proportional breasts, graceful neck.

When Julia passed by Marie in the hall or sat next to her in a class or the library, Marie ignored her. Worse. She shunned her, looking through Julia as if she were less than air. But to everyone else, Marie was the top student, drama geek, cheerleader, scholar society, homecoming princess; someone everyone wanted to hate but couldn't. Too quiet, too nice, too pretty, too perfect.

Ducking her head down, her eyes on the carpet, Julia slipped by her mother's rogue's gallery of the past, the innumerable photos of Julia at various stages and ages. Celebrations, birthdays, graduations, all neatly framed. In the bathroom, she closed the door, leaving the light off, not wanting to see her face in this mirror. She went to the bathroom, washed her hands, splashed water on her face, and then washed it, too, with a special cleanser her mother left for her use. The whole time, she kept her eyes shut, but the problem was, she could still see everything, even with them closed.

After lunch, Julia helped her mother clean up the mess of the lasagna plates and then headed downtown in the Mercedes for some supplies. Together, they decided a weekend would be the right length for a visit. Connie was going to go back to work on Monday, and there was no reason for Julia to use up her vacation time.

"Great," Deb said in her voice mail. "Drive carefully. And oh, don't forget to fill up the tank."

Watch out for floods, Arturo texted. Stay away from dams. Carry a life vest. Do you have one of those little hammers for breaking open the window if the car is submerged?

Julia was sure he wasn't kidding.

"Don't worry. I'll keep you posted," Connie said. "I'll be fine. You know me."

It was true. Early motherhood, sudden divorce, tragedy, illness, chaos. Connie almost always bounced back, into her house, where she would whip up a meal. But there were some things food couldn't fix.

Now, Julia swooshed past Hooker Oak Park, headed toward the Safeway for some salad makings and garlic bread. Chico was depressed by so much gray sky. The town had recently been ranked the seventh most miserable city to live in country-wide, the highest (or lowest scoring) in California. All this a big duh! to anyone who had grown up there.

Julia made a left on East Avenue, and in minutes, she was at the high school intersection, stopped at the red light. She'd missed the five-year reunion and was currently ignoring invitations to sign up for the tenth next year. She'd seen none of her old friends from high school for years, except on Facebook. But after accepting friend requests, she hid anyone who reminded her of anything. And everyone reminded her of everything.

Her heart sped up, her palms sweating into the leather steering wheel cover. She looked over at the large lawn in front of the office, swearing she could hear kids laughing and the bouncing of heavy balls: basketball, soccer. But it was a holiday or a teacher work day, the office, lot, and lawn empty. No kids, no cars, no parents. Behind her, someone honked, and before she knew what she was doing, Julia turned left into the parking lot, headed toward the drop-off site.

She pulled to a stop in the yellow pick-up zone—a place usually monitored by parents and school staff—and turned off the car.

The Mercedes was water tight and solid, the interior muffled, Julia an astronaut with a view, floating outside and above the school looking down before landing safely and intact. There was the office. There was the cafeteria. There was the gymnasium, the place where all the dances were held, even the junior and senior balls.

Opening the door, she put out a hand, palm up. The rain had stopped, the sky curling into itself and lifting, a sudden warmth filling the space where the rain had been. The air smelled tinny, like ozone, the before or after of lightning, but nothing rumbled in the clouds. Julia got out, beeped the door locked, and walked up to the wide, long swath of pavement, all of it covered by an overhang.

Julia walked past the office and then turned right, heading onto the campus. How many times had she done just that? Connie dropping her off, Julia running to find her friends. Desiree, Katy, Mara, and Sasha, the five of them a group, a pack, a posse. On the weekends, trips to the Chico Mall, the park, downtown. They gave each other sidelong glances in class, texted each other while holding their phones under their desks, and walked as a single entity through the halls.

Without Julia ever saying a word, they decided Marie was a bitch, and when she walked through the quad on some kind of personal cloud, they laughed, flicked their hair behind their shoulders. Julia had the move down, walking Marie's exact walk, *swish swish*, pushing her own hair back, *flick flick*.

"Oh, my ugly hair," Julia would say. "I don't know why it keeps hanging in front of my face."

"Get the pruning shears," Katy would add, all of them giggling.

In their laughter, Julia forgot about the snotty girl who peed on the floor. The girl who stole the pens. The girl who was invisible to those who counted.

During the long hot summers, they went to and then worked at the local pool, took trips to Tahoe and Stinson Beach, sat out on back decks, patios, and lawns and gossiped about everyone. Later, there were parties with girls, and then real parties with boys, too.

Now, Julia felt them next to her, even all these years later. In a crowd of twenty-seven-year old women, she could recognize them by the backs of their heads, their knees, their pinkie fingers, their laughter, whispers. All these years later, she could find them in a dark room by the smell of their favorite sodas.

After their high school graduation, all of them had reached out to her. Calls, emails, texts. Katy even wrote a letter. Sasha came by with her mother. But Julia never spoke to any of them, not once, not since.

Somewhere, laughter, the sound echoing against the wet walls. A boy on a bike zipped past her, his tires whirring on the slick cement.

Julia kept walking, her legs moving automatically, taking her back, right there, the corner of the gymnasium. Where had she been standing? Here? No, here. Next to the planter with the palm trees, all of them exactly the same but taller.

"Can you give me a ride home?" Marie had asked, surprising Julia who was waiting alone in the empty hall for Matthew who'd wandered off with two other boys to smoke some pot. Inside the gym, the last of the music banged against the ceiling and walls. Parents patrolled the wrong side of the gym, assuming kids would wander off into the parking lot for sex or drugs instead of hiding in the classroom hallways.

"What?" Julia flushed at the assault, her reaction when she saw Marie, which hadn't been often this semester, a no-show at sports events and rallies. Maybe Marie had been studying abroad? Maybe she only had two classes and work study?

"A ride," Marie whispered. "I need to get to the police."

"Aren't you being a bit dramatic?" Her heart thrummed in her chest; this was the most she'd said to Marie since second grade.

Marie looked over her shoulder and then moved closer. "I need the police."

Julia looked around. "What for? Nothing's happening."

Marie started to say something but then looked down and pulled at her dress, trying to cover her chest, her thighs. Her dress stretched oddly across her body, as if she'd put her arms in the neck or put it on backward. Or—or it was ripped, which it was, the red of the material shredded across the front. Had something happened with her boyfriend Jason? Besides, it was cold out. Why didn't she have one of her fancy wraps to drape over herself like a movie star?

"Just call your mom." Julia stepped back. "She'll come get you."

"I can't talk to her."

"I don't have my car," Julia said, looking away, her throat tight. "I don't even have my phone. I came with Matthew Denny. You probably don't even know who he is."

"Can he drive me?"

Julia turned to face her full-on, her hands on her hips. "No, he can't drive you. It's Senior Ball. Jesus. Where are all your special friends? Where's Jason? He can't be hard to find. Probably in the middle of the dance floor right now with all his football pals."

Marie shook her head. "Please."

"Go ask one of the parents. Have them call 911 if it's such an emergency, not that I see one." Julia's resolve tightened inside her like metal, her chest pulsing with twelve years of anger. Marie had let her steep in her own pee. She'd let Julia's nose run all over her face. Marie hadn't helped her one bit, ignoring Julia for the rest of their lives. Now she wanted a ride home?

"I don't have my phone. He—"

"I'm seriously surprised you'd ask me of all people," Julia said. "I'm not going to help you with anything."

"I'm sorry," Marie said. "I really am."

"It's too late."

Without looking at Marie again, Julia walked up the hallway and found Matthew by smell, the pot wafting. She took a hit, pulled him toward the parking lot, and they went home and had sex on her mother's family room couch, quietly. Matthew snuck out Sunday morning but was back Sunday night for BBQ. All of Julia's friends were there, Connie flushed with the pleasure of feeding so many. Everyone's parents came later, too, for dessert and wine.

It wasn't until Monday afternoon they heard Marie was missing, the school whirling with rumors: a runaway, an older boyfriend, Los Angeles, where she would become an actress.

Julia hung on to those stories, let them carry her through graduation and into summer. She traveled with her friends, worked at the pool, hung out with Matthew, their connection beginning to fray in anticipation of their upcoming separation to attend colleges at opposite sides of the country. But in July, two fishermen found Marie's body in Lake Shasta, still wearing her prom dress or what was left of it. It wasn't her date Jason who had done it. He thought Marie had stood him up. He'd been stag that night, dancing with everyone in a mosh pit and drinking from a flask of whiskey and passing out at a friend's. All corroborated.

No, it had been Marie's mother's boyfriend, a man who had lived with Marie since before second-grade, who'd been molesting her all along. That night, she'd finally tried to put a stop to it, but he'd followed her to the dance, attacking her in the parking lot. When she'd come across Julia, she was finally ready to tell someone.

And Julia didn't listen, Julia had said no. She'd said it more than once. And then she'd walked away.

Of course, he'd found Marie later, and then he'd strangled her and tossed her body in the lake. He'd never been found, his last known whereabouts Bellingham, Washington. He was probably living in Alaska under an assumed name. A man no one would ever guess was a rapist pedophile murderer.

"I never knew a thing. I had no idea," Marie's mother told the police and reporters.

"Oh, Marie," Julia said now. "I'm so sorry."

But Marie was silent. Julia put a hand on the cool gymnasium wall and conjured Marie, beautiful even in her ripped dress, messed hair, and smeared makeup. Beautiful as she pleaded for help to a girl who hated her for a second-grade mistake, a childish, stupid thing.

"I'll take you to the police station," Julia said. "I'll wait with you. I'll listen to the whole story. I'll protect you."

She imagined turning to see that horrible man emerge from the gloom, a swamp beast, a mastodon. She would run at him with her fists, beating him away from the act that would end Marie's life and ruin her own. She wanted to scratch and hit and kick.

"Run!" she'd call to Marie. "Go!"

Dazed and smoky, Matthew would emerge from the hall. But he would get it, yanking Marie to safety. Parents guarding the wrong part of the school would come running, using their cell phones to call the right people.

Julia would tell them all what the man was doing, and a stronger bigger man would wrestle him to the ground. The darkness would flood with flashing blue and red lights and fill with sirens.

And then, Julia would never have to tell her mother, which she did the day story came out. She wouldn't have to see her mother's face, the way it crumpled as they sat at the dining room table, the July 16th newspaper spread out in front of them with its awful news. The way she looked differently at Julia, as if she were an imposter who had posed as a good person all these years.

"Oh," her mother had said, eyes and mouth in a shape of horror she couldn't articulate.

"I didn't know," Julia had told her, leaning over the newspaper and the story, Lake Shasta under one arm, Marie's graduation photo under the other.

"Oh," her mother repeated, reaching out a hand, placing it on Julia's forearm but not squeezing. "Oh."

"Marie," Julia called out now. "Where are you?"

Even as she called, Julia knew exactly where Marie was: in the spaces between Deb's relentless emails, the airtight Mercedes, the boxes of crackers eaten over the white hole of the kitchen sink, the flooded middle of California, the water breaking down dams. Marie was what was not said in every conversation. She was the name unspoken in each sentence Julia said to her mother.

The Happiness

When Frank's younger wife left him and then Claire's second husband died, their two sons put them in a home, a house, in Phoenix. A house the older son Greg had bought and lived in, moved out of, rented, cleared out, and then organized for them, Claire and Frank, his divorced parents. Divorced as in forty-five years divorced. Divorced twice-as-long-as-they'd-been-married divorced.

No one ever imagined this ridiculous scenario, assuming that Frank's second wife Joanna would live for decades, taking care of him as he moldered in his soggy diapers. But seventy-year-old Joanna was now outliving him just fine in Manhattan with her fifty-eight-year old husband.

The good news for Claire was that she was strong. Walking on her own two feet. Unmedicated, at least for now.

"All there! My parts mostly intact," Claire would tell anyone who'd listen, not that anyone did anymore. Those who used to—some avidly—had died, one by one. Her bridge group, her theater club, her best friends from back when her children were actually children. The women she'd sat pool and courtside with. Carpool, Boy Scouts, 4H. Last spring, her first and last friend Bernadine died—both of them young as foals when they met over sixty years ago.

Claire had made do. Strolling around her neighborhood, talking to the dog walkers and parents with perambulators. She spoke to and emailed each of her three children weekly. Opened their "care" packages, the same way they must have opened hers when they were away at college. What did they send her? Goji berries, flax seeds, probiotics.

She drove to her hair appointments, the grocery store, the library. Pedicure now and again because it was tough getting to that real estate these days. Marie, the gal who did her toes, always had some gossip about the clientele, most of whom had been going to the shop for years. Careful with her shiny new polish, Claire arrived home a smidge smug.

But there had been mishaps. Her car flooded because she hadn't been able to close the sunroof. The emergency brake she thought was off wasn't, Claire pulling over to a flume of acridity and billowing smoke. She stopped using her cell phone, her computer, even her television, all electronics too confusing. Most of this was understandable. But then she'd had that accident in the gym. Really, it had been the trainer's fault. That bar slipped right out of its moorings. Nothing to do with her. But after that public disaster, the MRI, the blood work, the neuro consult. The conferencing. The car, parked for good in the garage. Lots of crying, mostly hers.

Frank had been worse off. Neighbors called when they hadn't seen him in a week. Turned out he was holed up on a leather recliner with a box of Saltines and a bottle of Knob Creek, curtains closed, lights off. Watching those reruns of 70s shows. At least he knew how to use the remote. Joanna MIA, the neighbor called their elder son's number on the wall: Emergency Contact.

So there the former spouses were. Eighty-eight and ninety, hanging on like crabs, despite the earlier heart attack and cancer, bum hips, hip replacements, knee replacements, and loneliness. In the mornings, a slow stroll around the block. Puzzles and lunch and long naps. In the evenings, lugubrious card games on the patio, hummingbirds buzzing by like warplanes. Sometimes, TV, but usually, both of them shuffled off to bed early, both on the arm of an aide, one who would sleep in the third bedroom, baby alarms on her bedside table. The good news thus far was all the aide had to deal with was a snoring duet.

Their younger son Chris filled the place with needed medical-type equipment (furniture that cranked up and down, clicking and clacking). Claire's daughter Jane was hard pressed to help her half-brothers, both of whom were in their mid-sixties. This girl/woman, born when Claire was forty-four, had been a trouble-maker, a wild child, a free spirit, but through therapy, rehab, and lots of higher education, was finally a full professor at a small university in Tacoma, Washington. But on that salary, all she could do was chip in to pay for the home health aides, two women (plus a relief aide on the weekends) who took turns, day and night. Also, there was the housecleaner, the gardener, the pool guy. The groceries and drug store supplies came by delivery truck. At night, Claire heard the automatic sprinklers whirring.

How did poor people grow old and die? Claire wondered. Not that she or Frank were rich anymore, but their sons were.

Right now, Frank—her ex-husband, her first husband, her former spouse, the father of two of her three children—and she sat in matching rockers on the swath of slate patio. The chairs creaked in rhythm as they moved a gentle back and forth, back and forth. Outside, the sandy sky filled with purple, the sun a slim flat line on the horizon dotted with saguaro cacti and smooth blobs of boulders. Without looking at him, she could tell that his eyes were almost closed, but not quite, his slitted vision taking in the last of the day. How many times had she turned to him during school performances or sporting events and flushed with anger that he wasn't paying attention?

"You don't know what your own children are doing!" she'd hiss.

He'd raise a hand, say, "It's 3 to 1. I know." On the field, the various balls would careen between players, a score here, there. Cheers and clapping. All the while, Frank with his irritating Buddha behavior.

"I see everything," he'd intone, suddenly standing up to whoop as Greg or Chris shot, hit, scored. He'd pat backs, take a swig of Bud, and then go back to his inscrutability.

"You're killing me," she'd whisper.

"My objective," he'd say.

At some point, Claire knew he meant it.

The good news, Claire realized a few months after the divorce was finalized, was that he hadn't killed her. Not her body, anyway. Her heart took a beating. Her brain. Her blood pressure. How not? Just forty and deserted by an uncommunicative husband. Off he went to the arms of his beautiful twenty-something mistress. There Claire was with two pubescent boys and saddlebags. All she needed was a bridle and a cowboy.

No cowboy, much less businessman, appeared on the imminent horizon, so eventually, she started going to the singles parties at the local Presbyterian church. Punch bowl, tables for conversation, bad music from the 40s and 50s to dance to. A general junior high dance feel, where even the wallflowers had been pulled from their sticky corners. What else to do? So she danced until the party was over, and then went back every weekend, ignoring her sons' eye-rolling.

Truth was, though, she had to deal with the mirror. Her clothing. No wonder Frank had kept his eyes slit as she disrobed night after night. What had she been thinking? She bemoaned her ugly white Maidenform bras, and after her second singles party, she tossed all her lingerie, buying new bras that stretched and gleamed with shiny synthetic fabrics. Underwear that didn't go all the way up to her navel. Pantyhose with tummy-tucking support. Then she found one dress, two, both revealing she still had an hourglass fig-ure, despite the two children and recent unhappiness.

Claire didn't meet her second husband Rich at a party, but she met a woman by the punchbowl who introduced her to Rich a few months later at a cocktail party held off-grid from the singles party circuit. A week afterward, he picked her up in his big Buick, that long bench seat onto which she slid easily. All that polyester under her dress.

Two years after that first date, she and Rich married. The di-vorce had left her the house and the boys, who refused to go to New York to visit their father, and didn't, not until they graduated from college and managed to forgive him. She had a new husband, her own car, and child support, and when she and Rich got back from their honeymoon in Oahu, she found a job. Oh, nothing that she'd studied in school. Her skills were long gone, technical in-formation obsolete. But she took the test at the local library and was hired. Request unit. Calling around the county for best-selling or obscure texts. Reading the teletype machine for crucial district information. Chatting with her co-workers. Going out to lunch. At night, she and Rich talked about their jobs over dinner. It was all going so well, but then the pregnancy. Unplanned—wasn't she ready to go through the change, just as her mother had at for-ty-three? Hadn't she felt done as done could be?

Um, no. Jane was born the month Claire turned forty-five.

Just before her due date, Claire quit the library and dug around for all her baby supplies, long buried in the garage shelving unit. About a second after the nursery was ready, Jane came, squalling, pink, and perfect.

All that life seemed, well, a lifetime ago.

Now behind her and Frank, Marta, the aide who stayed with them five of seven nights, clattered in the kitchen, talking on her cell phone to her son in Juárez, Mexico. Night took over the sky with purples, blues, and black. Stars pricked the sky with tiny fingers. In the distance, coyote yips and someone's irritating two-stroke machine (motorcycle?).

"*Mi'jo*," Marta was saying. "*Vengase para aca.*"

Frank shook his head. "That boy won't come to this country."

"Why not?" Claire asked. Neither of them knew Jesús, Marta's son.

"His mother's a busybody. Bossy. Just listen. Telling him what to do. Move here. Go to night school. Get a job. Get citizenship. *Blah, blah, blah.* If she didn't wipe my ass sometimes, I'd tell her a thing or two."

Claire glanced at him, hearing his comments from decades ago. "Leave the kid alone, god dammit," he'd said after Greg stole a rocket kit from the five and dime downtown. "He's got the store owner and the sheriff on his ass. Scare him into next week."

"Maybe the school counselor," Claire had said, turning away to her dressing table. "He might need someone to talk to."

Frank slammed his fist on the nightstand. "He doesn't need any goddamn counselor. He needs to stop the bullshit and grow up!"

All those years, he'd told her she'd coddled both boys. Overdone the birthday parties. Tried too hard. Thought too much about every little thing. Just like Marta, Claire guessed. She wanted to stand up and walk into the kitchen and tell Marta that Greg turned out to be happy. And rich, by the way. Also, four kids, four grandchildren.

Take that, Frank, you putz.

And yes, she'd take the phone from Marta's hand and say, "Jesús, get yourself up here."

Busybody indeed.

Marta hung up and cursed a little in Spanish, flicking on the water to do the dinner dishes. The kitchen lights gleamed on the slick shrub leaves, all varieties unfamiliar to Claire, except the butterfly brush. In the light, the spears glowed violet.

"You never wanted anyone telling you what to do."

Frank made a sound at the back of his throat, the kind only an old man or a goat could. "Did not."

Claire snorted. "Not everyone is like you."

"Shame that, huh? World a better place."

As if. God, what arrogance! And at his age, when all the world wanted was for him to be gone. And soon enough, he would be. Her, too. Their boys would come back to the house and take it over, pack it up, fire the aides, sweeping up the small matter of their entire lives. And still Frank was who he was. Her, too, though of course she thought that was preferable. Nicer. She was the nicer one. Parent. Person. At least, she hadn't been the one to leave.

Claire pushed back in her rocker a bit harder, the next rock a prolonged creeeak. "Frank, some people actually want a little guidance."

All these years later, anger. Another husband, job, child, and she still wanted to do her first husband some violence, at least verbally. But at his chuckle, she sensed she'd missed her mark.

Creak, creak, their chairs moved but went nowhere. *Splash, splash,* the water went down the drain.

Frank patted one of his own bony knees and let out a throaty sigh. "I should have listened to you forty years ago, Claire. Damn if I didn't pay attention. Maybe if I had, neither of us would be right here now."

"We'd be old still."

"But maybe not old in this way."

"Maybe not," Claire said, wondering where the turns came that made this this happen.

A hoot owl hooted and then flew its dark body across the backyard.

If only Claire had listened. But to whom? And to what? Maybe the owl. But even it was gone.

It was hard not to worry when she and Frank were at their doctors' office. Kate, their daytime caretaker, sat next to Claire, reading a magazine, occasionally glancing up at the television that hung from the ceiling. Claire kept her eyes on her thighs, her hands on top, skin veiny and spotted. Inside the examination room with his doctor, Frank was undergoing poking and prodding. She was worried for him, of course, but as she stroked the casual fabric of her pants, she knew she was mostly worried for herself. What if there was something very wrong with his heart or lungs? His kidneys, spleen, or liver? Any of his crucial systems? He'd be whisked to the hospital or care. Their sons would fold up the house and send Claire to care, too, both of them locked up. Or down. Finished. Lined up with the bungled or the botched, sitting in their wheelchairs and confined like the living dead they were.

"He'll be fine." Kate closed her magazine and flopped it on the table. "It's just a checkup. You know that."

Claire wanted to swallow in agreement and relief, but her tongue wouldn't cooperate. So she nodded instead.

"You both are in amazing shape," Kate said. "Trust me, I have seen everything."

"I don't feel very amazing," Claire admitted. "All bones and stretchy everything else."

Kate tapped her head. "Both of you are keeping it together."

The door opened from the inner office, and Kate stood, ready to help Frank, who needed to book another appointment. Claire stared at him, the way he shuffled as he walked. His back a bit humped, his hair a whirl of sparse white, his eyes squinty (and not because he was being inscrutable. Because he couldn't see). How could this old man be the boy she met when she was not quite twenty-two, living in San Francisco, just graduated from Cal?

There he came, bounding up the boarding room steps, his eyes shining, his hair thick, dark, and curly, his shoulders broad.

"Hey, there," he'd said, pulling up short, breathing a bit hard. "How ya doing?"

Claire had felt every single part of herself still. At his question, she realized she hadn't been doing well at all. Aside from her married supervisor who harassed her in the breakroom and elevators, she was lonely at her work as a bench chemist at the naval lab. Her sorority sisters and girlfriends at Cal had gone into marriages right after graduation. Only she had turned down her former boyfriend's marriage proposal—a lawyer who adored her—because she hadn't adored him, but she'd regretted her decision during the long evenings after work. She bit into her grilled cheese sandwiches and sipped her bowls of Campbell's tomato soup. What an idiot. Clearly, she could have made do, what with Larry's family house in Carmel, his apartment on Nob Hill, his ambition that might have led them to Sacramento and then maybe even Washington, D.C.

That's what she got for going into the sciences.

"What are you thinking?" her mother had asked when Claire came home for Christmas break. "Chemistry?"

Claire had been good at math in high school. Chemistry was similar but with molecules. They wanted her to declare a major, but maybe her mother was right. What had she been thinking?

But when Claire saw this shining young man, breathing a little hard after running up five flights of stairs, she knew. She'd been waiting. For him. For his proposal that would come six months later. For the house in the suburbs and her two sons. For the country club summers and dinner parties and friends around the pool drinking g and t's from highball glasses. For the vacations to Waikiki Beach and Lake Tahoe. For the family dinners and holidays, his family in San Diego and the trips back and forth. Those shopping trips in Union Square with his mother Adele and sister

Susan. And mostly, his stomach against her back, his arm around her waist. His heat. Every night.

Sometimes he'd turn to her—years after that first stairwell visitation. It didn't matter where. Their house. A park. A movie theater. And in a quick crack of time, she'd see him as he'd been. Aimed right for her.

How could that beautiful man have left her and their two children? How could he have fought over every single cent he begrudgingly sent them? How could he have transformed into this shuffling old coot in front of her, his left pant leg hem drooping under his scuffed shoe?

As they all walked out of the medical building lobby, Claire caught her reflection in the mirror behind reception. There she was. A shock of white hair, a face like a crumpled shopping bag, body like an origami coat hanger. Not even close to the girl standing before the boy on the stairwell, the girl waiting for her life to start.

The entire afternoon plan consisted of a puzzle. Currently, Claire and Frank were working on a ridiculous thousand-piece jigsaw of the United States. The pieces tiny, the completed object supposedly three feet by two, the thing would barely fit on the game table. As Claire stared at the shiny colors, she wondered if by sending such a time-consuming puzzle monster, Jane thought she could keep her mother busy and alive.

All fifty states, each full of important symbols, icons, flora, and fauna. California—according to the box—replete with the Hollywood sign, the Golden Gate Bridge, and the Sierra Nevada mountain range. Texas with The Alamo. New York with the Empire State Building. Etcetera. Worse, the puzzle was shaped like the country, no square edges to find and frame. No real way to feel productive.

"This is too damn hard." Frank flicked the pile of yellow they'd created and then reached out to unknown territory, one long index fingernail scratching a piece the color of mortadella (A horse? A deer?). All the damn flowers. The red pile was mostly flowers, too. States were big with flowers. At least California had orange, but even the poppies seemed yellow. Hard to put them in the right piles.

Outside, Ramón blew leaves into brown piles. Marta had arrived for her shift and was changing the sheets, the whir of the bed mechanisms cranking up and down, up and down. Something in the oven smelled oniony.

"Why did you do it?" Claire asked.

"Damn piece is yellow," Frank said. "Where else should it go?"

"Why didn't you tell me earlier?" Claire asked. "Why didn't you give me a chance?"

Frank pushed the piece toward the pile. "Have at it."

"Don't be dense. I mean about us. The boys. Our family."

Frank shook his head, three strands of white long hair floating over his forehead. One summer, they'd taken the boys to Cancún, before it became what it was to be, big hotels and fancy restaurants. They stayed in a casita by a white sand beach, all of them eating in a larger house for their meals. The boys played in the sand and splashed all day. Claire swam in the water and read a dozen paperbacks in the shade, and Frank built sandcastles and tossed balls with the boys. His hair grew long, his skin tanned. At night in their hard double bed, he made love to her in a way she thought was real.

"I couldn't keep doing it," he said.

"What? Me?"

He shook his head, pressed the hair down on his skull. "The happiness."

Claire couldn't breathe or think, though she did feel parts of

Florida under her right hand. Oranges, Miami, the Gulf. Parts of her she'd thought had gone into hibernation panged. Sorrow. Anguish. Despair.

All that happiness.

Now he sat back and looked at her, his eyes and mouth pushed back into his face, muscles slack, his lips parted. "You can't hide. You can't sit in another room. I had to leave it."

"I don't understand." Claire's heart beat in her throat, her ears. She clasped her hands, pressing them together.

"So much easier to have less. It doesn't hurt—"

"After Joanna took off, they found you hunched like a squirrel over a box of crackers," Claire spit out. "Are you telling me that didn't hurt?"

Again, Frank shook his head. "It didn't. I was just waiting to die. But instead, here I am. Back where I started. With you. Probably the only way I could have managed it."

Claire stared at him, not understanding one word he was saying. Marta bustled down the hall, clutching sheets. "Dinner in fifteen minutos," she said.

"You're saying you wanted this?"

"Who else should I die with?" he said.

Claire wanted to stand, curl her hands under the edge of the game table, and flip it and the puzzle up and over, the country falling to literal pieces. She wanted to storm out of the house, just as Frank had decades before, in a righteous tempest. She wanted to cut him to the bone with words, about how Rich had been three times the husband. A better father, too. How Rich's money had helped fund the moves to Phoenix. How he was sitting in Rich's chair. As if Frank could begin to fill that seat!

All of the decades of taunts and slurs and provocations roared up her throat, gunning their terrible engines. She'd waited all this time to say them, and now was her chance.

Claire had given him everything. Herself. Her body. Her life. Her anger. Her suffering. Her tears. And her joy. Her hope. Her surprise. Yes, her surprise. That she could have what she wanted, even when she'd thought life would be lonely nights in a boarding house. That moment on the stairwell, she'd handed it all over, willingly. And yes, with the understanding of how dangerous the proposition.

Here, she'd said. Take it all. Take it so much that it hurts. Take it so much that when you leave, I'll be left with only your absence.

She'd done it before. So she knew how to give herself to the surprise of Frank, and she could do it again. After all, who else could she die with? Who else but this man on the stair, the old coot with the bad hem.

Claire exhaled, leaned forward, put her shaking fingers on the mysterious yellow piece, pushed it to the pile. Georgia? Alabama, maybe? California? No, Arizona. Some yellow petaled flower of Phoenix. Here. Here.

Don't Forget About Me

Number Three lumbers toward Tacie, pushes away a palm frond, rounds the chair, and pulls away his jacket as he sits, the restaurant chair creaking. He breathes hard and shallow, as if he just took a break from filling sand bags for a flood. He smells sweet, like dried cranberries or strawberry Jell-O.

Tacie smiles and wishes she could spot her friend Diane, who sits somewhere in this dark restaurant watching her own number three head toward her.

"Hey," Number Three says, and Tacie reads his name tag: Rick. Rick in red ink.

Rick is likely the largest man she's ever met in person. He sits wide-legged so his enormous belly can perch on his lap underneath his Hawaiian shirt. But he seems happy, if a bit sweaty, his forehead and upper lip glistening.

"I won't make jokes about you not going anywhere." He wipes his brow with a handkerchief, stuffs it in one pocket, and takes his dating scorecard out of another. "I'm sure you've heard it already. But the ladies get to sit while the guys make the rounds."

"I have heard that," Tacie says. She wants to say more things about not going anywhere. For one, her dating life, here in this dimly lit restaurant among the bungled and the botched, the sad and hopeless and despairing. She, first in line for all the terrible adjectives. She wants to point out to Rick that even though the men are moving from table to table at the sound of the bell, no one has made any progress. Who meets the love of his or her life at a speed dating event? What is this event but an excuse to go out and pretend to be living? It looks like moving forward but really, Tacie knows, it's two steps back.

Rick settles and looks at her name tag. "So, Tacie. Is that right?"

"Stacie without an 's,'" Tacie says.

As he smiles, his eyes disappear in the valleys between cheeks and forehead, but then they're back again, dark and intent.

"So, Tacie," Rick says. "Tell me about yourself."

Tacie has related these things twice before and now settles into her narrative. "I teach English," she says. "High school."

"I better watch my grammar," Rick jokes, and she doesn't tell him that's the third time a man has said those very words tonight.

"Don't worry," Tacie says. "I didn't bring my red pen."

That's the third time she's said that, too.

"What do you do?"

"I make hot tubs," Rick says, and without willing it, an image of a naked Rick submerging into a large redwood round of steaming water fills Tacie's mind. There he is, moonlit, moon-sized, glowing white in the night, the water lapping around the mounded rock of his body.

"You make them?"

He nods. "Hand-crafted and custom. One-offs."

"Oh," Tacie says.

"So what brings you here?" he asks.

"Divorce," Tacie says. "And my friend Diane."

She waves her hand toward wherever Diane is sitting, all these small for-two tables nested in fronds, hidden by high-backed chairs and candle light. When she and Diane met at a school district teacher-training seminar ten years ago, Tacie was married. When Tacie first left her husband, Diane was in a relationship. But now, they're free to go to Wednesday night speed dating at the threadbare steak house.

"What do we have to lose?" Diane had said. "Come on! You've been sitting at home every night for months."

All true. So Diane signed them up, and Tacie donned the hopeful makeup and dress of the blind date.

"What about you?" she asks Rick.

"I want a partner," Rick says, looking at her, his eyes deeply brown, glinting in the small candle's flickering light. "It's hard to meet people when you're out in the field all day."

Now Tacie thinks of fields of wooden hot tubs in the middle of Iowa farmland, row upon row filled with large white, bobbing men. Here comes Rick in his tractor, ready to harvest.

"Hot tubs," Rick continues, "don't have much to say."

"That's how I feel when I look at my students," Tacie says. "Where can we meet anyone?"

For a moment, they watch each other, and then Rick shrugs. "The modern age. We're all so isolated in our own lives."

"Right," Tacie says, and just as she wishes she could evaporate like hot tub steam, the time bell rings.

Rick holds out his meaty hand, and Tacie takes it, trying not to react to the wetness against her fingers. She looks hard into Rick's eyes, forcing herself to not shudder, and nods instead. In his gaze, she sees his want and hope, and she sees her own, that same sad need that brought her right here to this lonely two-top with the tiny red candle for a night of five-minute introductions with men she wouldn't even conjure in her imagination.

What hits her as she stares at Rick is that she is Rick. She may not weigh 400 pounds, but she's no better. To the men who come to sit with her, she's as odd and wrong and weird and troubled as Eduardo and Steve and Rick. She's the forty-two-year-old woman with what? Too much eyeliner and slightly sagging breasts and hands starting to spot. She dresses too young, trying to be hip and sexy—the black knee-high boots were a mistake—when she's anything but. The men will go home and wonder what is wrong with them. Why had they wasted their evening talking with her?

"Nice to meet you, Rick," she says, trying to mean it.

"Same here," he says, letting go, pushing himself up, his stomach rising like a hot air balloon over the table. "Don't forget about me."

She nods. So far this evening, Rick is who she will remember most.

"Christ," Number Four says.

He sits down, his mouth open, his eyes trying to blink back the horror that Tacie herself now feels, her heart belting around her chest like a panicked rodent.

"What are you doing here?" she asks, knowing that it would be best to get up and leave, but she's not sure that she could stand up without tipping over the small table, the candle setting the tatty carpet ablaze.

"Gee, I'm not sure. Let me think. Maybe it's that my wife left me for no good reason and I'm trying to meet someone? I don't know. Call me stupid."

"But here? To this? Did you know I was coming?" she asks.

"Yeah, I'm stalking you. I signed up to do this shit instead of just going to your apartment."

Her almost ex-husband David shakes his head, blows out air—a dismissive sound she knows too well. He pushes back his thick, dark hair in that familiar one swipe, two swipe. A gesture she could mimic to win at charades. In fact, she could probably find David in a crowded room by feel and taste and touch and sound. Everything he does she knows by heart: as he stares at her, he interlaces the fingers of both hands and rests them on his lap, he cocks his head, a nerve under his left eye twitches. She lived with him for twenty-three years, and that's enough time to know that under the table, his legs are crossed at the ankle. He's wearing dark blue socks. Boxers, not briefs. He ironed his crisp Dockers and white shirt before he left home, but he didn't bother to shave because his handsome, freckled face is so sensitive, he can only shave three times a week.

"Anyway, you're here," he says. "Trolling for love."

Tacie feels heat flare from her cheeks to throat, odd continents of shame blooming from collarbone to ear. When she left David, she told him it wasn't about anyone else. She promised him there was no other man, and there wasn't, but in her heart she hoped there might be.

They hadn't had time for romance, not with Rory coming so quickly after they married. Not with the bills and the fights about the bills. Not with both their hopes dashed, neither of them knowing what the other's hopes actually were. David was always so angry, so tense. And now, just as so often during their marriage, he was tight and clenched, anger right there under the smooth surface of his skin.

"You left me for this? Really?"

Before she can reply, he says, "What are you going to do? Go out with Gigantor?"

"He was nice."

"Nicer than me? Better than me?" David asks, his voice raising. "You left me so you could sit here and talk to a man who could barely walk away."

"Shhh," Tacie says, her whole body flushing. Without meaning to, she looks toward the other tables for reaction to his yelling. "Diane made me come."

"She's here, too?" David throws himself back against the chair. "Great."

With that, he slumps and shakes his head. As he bites down

on his back molars, Tacie can see the anger in his clenched teeth, the once, twice of his hard molar bite, his jaw working as though he were chewing gum. Waiting, she sees the sadness, too, the eye twitch, the swallowing.

"Why did you decide to speed date?" Tacie asks.

"Why not?" he says, fingering the fake cyclamen on the table. "What else to do with the rest of my life?"

"Oh, for god's sake please," she says, but she can't really find her own indignation. The rest of his life, that life she'd sworn to witness. Sworn to while holding hands. Over and over again, by word and deed and action, the deal sealed by the number of years she'd stayed when she didn't want to. Her lies were her litany of guilt, the worry beads of terrible thought she kept in her pocket until bedtime when she could bring them out and finger every one.

"Please," he says, his voice a whisper. "Stop this."

Yes, she thinks, the failure of her evening hanging on her shoulders like a heavy coat. It would just be so easy. Finally, it would be over. All she has to do is stand up and take his hand, both of them leaving the speed dating arena and dating forever. They will go home and call their son at college. Rory would be overjoyed that the fighting and haggling and general emotional mayhem is over.

Without a word, David will lead her back to the bedroom, and she will sit on her side of the bed on the comforter she bought at the country store in Mendocino. She will take off her clothes and put them in her still-empty drawers. She will lay back and have the familiar, ordinary, and basically pleasant sex she's had for years with a man she knows. In less than half an hour, she'll be right back in the spot that took her years to leave.

Later, after more promises, they will go to better therapy that might actually work, join a monthly book club, and plant redbuds and rhododendrons in the backyard. They will take neighborhood walks and go to cooking classes and travel every summer to Europe. In time, maybe ten years from now, these last two ravaged years will look like a rip perfectly repaired, the stitching almost invisible. In twenty-seven years, Rory and his wife and grown children and all Tacie's and David's extended family and dear friends will be toasting Tacie and David's fifty long years together, separation and speed dating a forgotten nightmare.

Tacie stares at her still husband, so known and clear, even in the ways she doesn't like: his sarcasm, his anger, his inability to see the important, true thing about her that even she cannot identify. But who will ever find it? Who will ever understand? David knows her better than any other person on the planet. No one will ever understand her well enough to be this angry at her again. All she has to do is stand up and take his hand. No one but maybe Diane will say a word against it. Everyone will nod and agree, saying, "I always hoped you two would get back together."

The bell rings, and David leans closer. "Tacie," he says. "You don't have to do this. You can still come home."

All she has to do is go. Someone moves the palm frond but steps back when Tacie jerks up. She looks back to David, slammed back into the reality of the dark room, yanked away from the happy ending she will never live into.

"No," she says, and she makes herself look at him, this man she watched age from a still-boy to a man, her husband, the father of her child. She wants to reach out to touch him, but she knows she's given away the right. Tacie holds his gaze as his anger takes over any bit of tenderness that might have survived if this night had never happened.

The bell rings again, and David pulls his hands off the table and pushes the chair back, the sound a viscous scrape on the wood floor.

He stands over her, and some part of her wishes he would make a scene. Now he could yell, throw the stupid candle, call her names. He might pick her up by her shoulders and shake her bone by bone, spitting in her face as he screams out his pain.

But all he says is, "Enjoy your night. I hope you're the most popular girl in the room."

The table shakes as he leaves, the fronds flash and flicker as he pushes past. On the table, David's score-card rocks like an empty boat. And in the rocking back and forth, she sees all that's missing in everything.

Tacie tries to follow his progress in the restaurant, strangely hoping that he'll stay and meet someone, but she can't track him, can't hear a heavy, slammed restaurant door, doesn't see a lone woman waiting for David, a woman who doesn't yet know these next five minutes will be a blessed relief.

Number Five appears, a short blond man holding his score card tight.

"Hi," he says. "I'm Jeff."

Later, after the last man has sat at the final table, Tacie waits for Diane out front, her friend chatting with her Number Ten, a man who didn't wait for the score-cards to be tabulated or a call to see if both parties were interested. Smitten, Number Ten stayed seated at Diane's table long after the second bell, and as Tacie looks back into the restaurant foyer, it's clear by Diane's big smile that her friend is not upset by this breach.

Tacie clutches her coat and purse and walks a few feet to sit on the wooden bench at the side of the door, staring out to the emptying parking lot. It's almost fall, the summer giving way to cooler nights. Couples and singles, servers and cooks just off work walk briskly to their cars or to the bus stop on the corner of Broadway and Main. She's already scanned for David's Lexus, but she knows he's long gone. From the cars remaining in the lot, it appears that Diane's Number Ten might drive either a minivan or a Toyota sedan of some kind. Not a doctor, but not unemployed, either.

The door swings open, and she almost stands, but she sees that it's not Diane and Number Ten, but Rick. Tacie sits back down keeps watching him, wondering if she should say something, hoping he won't or, maybe, hoping he will see her on the bench. But Rick is all business.

With one hand, he clutches the railing, taking each step carefully and slowly, one, two, three, four. His shoes have thick rubbery soles, and she can hear their squishy groans as he makes his way down to the paved entryway. Once he lands, he adjusts the jacket he put on over his Hawaiian shirt and takes a deep, relieved breath which Tacie can hear from where she sits. Then, eyes forward and with a slow, thoughtful gait, Rick heads to the remaining cars, veering toward the minivan.

Something in the way he walks makes Tacie imagine him how he might have been as a boy, fifteen, on the football field, jogging back to the huddle. Sure, he was heavy even then—a linebacker—but he was powerful, shoulders square as they are now, arms moving with a firm, serious swing. At some point later in his life—ten, maybe fifteen years—he let go of hope, faith, or control.

Tacie can't take her eyes off him. All evening long, he's moved forward, and on, and through, not giving up, not stopping. Not one single issue in his life has prevented him from driving all the way here tonight, and not one thing will keep him from trying until he finds that partner, the woman who sees him in the true way he can't see himself.

If all Tacie does from the rest of her life is try half as hard as Rick does now, she will be okay. She's not half the person he is—literally—and things will be so much easier for her. One step, two, three, and go.

Rick gets in his car, a hauling, yanking process. The minivan tilts slightly towards the driver's side after he gets in. The van starts, its lights illuminating the front of the restaurant, with Tacie flowered in the yellow glare. She thinks of what she will say if he pulls up and rolls down his window, but Rick accelerates slowly, making a smooth turn in his titling minivan and drives away from her, out of the lot, and into the sparse flow of the ordinary midweek traffic.

The Dry Years

Pippa sometimes forgot the joke Em told them when times were strange. What was it? That saying from the British comedy show in the 70s?

On the YouTube clips, the audience burst into laughter when the red-robed, crucifix-wearing priests broke through the flimsy set door and surprised the family eating dinner, the employees at the quarterly meeting, the primary school students learning fractions.

Em had repeated the expression in the face of four-mile long traffic jams, surprise tax bills, leaking toilets, raccoons in the basement. She said it when Mattie brought home bad grades or Pippa forgot to clean her room. Em would cross her arms, give them a pretend-stern look, and repeat it slowly, her voice a fake deep. "No one expects the Spanish Inquisition."

She said it at the very end when nothing was funny.

Pippa agreed. No one expects extermination, even though that's the deal with living in the first place. Disease, rancid old age, fascist regime, pogrom, tornado, earthquake.

You just don't expect it, is all.

Pippa refilled her coffee mug and sat back down at her computer, waiting for someone to respond to their boss Sue's rant about the lack of donations. She had colleagues she'd never met in person and who were images (sometimes pixilated) on a computerized meeting screen, words in messages, emails, and texts, and/or voices on infrequent phone calls. She'd met Sue once, when Pippa interviewed for the data position at Nature Now, two days before moving to Hilo three years ago. The only thing they all had in common was the slogan: *Remember the Sloths.*

After a pause, Royce from Minneapolis, the guy with the profile pic that looked like a 1980s Marlon Brando, said, "The school shooting diverted the flow."

"Jesus," Sue said. "Of course it did."

"The NRA picked up the slack. Their donations tripled last month?" Royce said, a lift at the end of his sentence. Even over the internet, Royce looked red as sin.

The ConfAll link screen went silent. All sidebar messages stopped. Apparently the NRA was worse than the school shooting itself.

Pippa, a familiar, uncomfortable feeling in her chest, coughed the scratch from her throat. "But it's a new month."

"Be that as it may," Sue began, "we are way down in legacy donations not to mention tip jar giving."

The conversation began to roll again. Pippa relaxed in her chair as she listened to a meeting that was happening twenty-five hundred miles away and three hours ahead in time.

"As long as you meet your deliverables," Sue had said to Pippa's question about working remotely on the nonprofit's data team. "You can live anywhere. Just get your work done."

So that's what Pippa had done for twenty-five dollars an hour, money that wouldn't go very far in Hawaii if she didn't have her caretaking job. After two months with Nature Now and at Sue's repeated request, Pippa had posted a headshot on her page, email, and links. By then, Sue had forgotten what Pippa looked like anyway, so Pippa got away with using a photo of her older sister Mattie. In essentials, they looked the same, so Pippa really couldn't blame busy Sue for not noticing. Blonde-haired, brown-eyed, oval-faced, darkly eyebrowed. Prominent cheekbones, pixie chins.

The photo Pippa snagged was from Mattie's wedding. The sun glinted behind her sister, her whole face alight. Mattie had married her true love, Walter, and moved to Portland to open up their very own restaurant. Last year, they had their first child, named Genevieve, after Em.

"You haven't even pretended to want to visit," Mattie said every time she called, which was at least twice a week. "You haven't invited us to come see you. I miss you."

"You can't leave the restaurant," Pippa replied each time because it was true.

In front of her, the computer images flickered like a flock of starlings.

"I'll search for all the maybes," Pippa said into the silence of the online meeting space. "Those who were encouraging on the cold calls but didn't donate."

"Social media," Royce added. "Barrage."

"Do it," said Sue.

And then, like that, the meeting collapsed into nothing but air.

Outside, the air was crisp and filled with the calls from invasive bird species, the ones Pippa liked best for their colors and sounds: red-billed leiothrix, red-crested cardinals, Gambel's quail. Alone in the yard, she would answer the quail, calling out, *ha, ha, aha, aha, aha,* mimicking the slow, prolonged laugh.

"If you don't catch the seedlings," her landlord Nate told her when he explained the yard work, "the whole house will disappear. A three-bedroom house is no match for ten acres of wet Hawaiian soil."

"That's not the plants' fault." Pippa tried to keep her voice light. "It's not like they asked to come here."

"Someone brought them," Nate said.

"They could have been stowaways," Pippa said. "On ships and in luggage."

"Or flung by storm."

"Trapped," Pippa added.

"Trying to escape," Nate said, laughing. "No rest for the wicked."

"It feels so arbitrary." She wondered how she could rip something whole and alive from the ground. She could almost hear the roots screaming.

"Everything is. But you can do it," Nate said. "You'll see."

Now, sweat trickled down her spine as she clipped and yanked, practiced now at plant murder.

"A gentleman's farm," Nate said during their first call. He had called from his dry-as-toast house in Santa Fe, New Mexico, where he'd already moved. "Keep the farm out of the house, and you can live there forever."

For two weeks, she wondered if Nate's ad on Craigslist had been a scam that would eventually find her a sex slave in an Illinois subdivision, but he was really Nate in Santa Fe who didn't want to sell his Hilo house, at least not yet. His closest neighbor was moving back to the mainland and couldn't watch the place anymore.

"Let's see where this artist thing goes," he told her.

Every month, he reported on the high and dry climate of the southwest and his wretched painting classes. "Watch out or I'll send my rejects home to Hilo."

But he never did.

Pippa plotted out her work, listed her tasks on a spreadsheet along with her work schedule. Today was ripping out the bastard jasmine, which was its actual name. Bastard jasmine. She sat on the warm, wet grass and pulled at the vines that scrambled over the hedges and across the lawn. The tubular flowers were bright crimson with yellow pistils, so pretty that she had two vases of them on the kitchen counter.

She'd taken the machete to the pampas grass yesterday, and tomorrow was about ripping out the rubbervine. Once a week, she sat on the mower and made perfect circles around the house, the thick, springy grass an orderly protection against the other flora that threatened to swallow it.

She made sure the catchment was catching and the cesspool didn't overflow or explode or whatever it was that cesspools did when things went horribly wrong. She kept an eye out for cockroaches and fire ants. Pippa battened down the hatches and closed the storm shutters against potential tsunamis, not that she or the house would survive one of those.

As best as possible, Pippa took care, as per agreement.

Wind pushed up out of the ocean and swirled across the tops of trees. Pippa hunkered on her haunches, throwing a wad of jasmine on the pile. The clouds overhead were black with rain but nothing was falling. On the house wall next to her, a gecko paused.

Em had taught her about birds. Plants, too. That's what she was doing at the very end as she and Pippa looked out the shattered window.

Blood trickled down her face, but Em pointed up. "Look at the branches. We're held between palms."

Em tried to smile, and Pippa stilled.

"Eucalyptus," Em said. "So green."

The long leaves hung down like claws, seed pods clicking on the car roof.

Mattie was 18 when it happened, old enough to be given charge of her thirteen-year-old sister. The judge appointed her custodian, even though it was clear she couldn't take care of herself, much less Pippa. Mattie stayed out late and came home early, sleeping till noon. She lost one job and then another. Her skin grew dry, her hair turned into magical dead straw. She weighed less than one hundred pounds, her knees as knobby as oranges. So Pippa made sure they ate dinner and the rugs were vacuumed. She paid the bills online and fed the animals.

After court appointed therapy, Mattie managed to crest up and over her "bad period" and signed Pippa up for SAT tutoring and helped her with college applications. Mattie rented the U-Haul and drove Pippa to Claremont College and went to freshman orientation with her. Pippa came home to Mattie during college breaks. Mattie was Pippa's family until Mattie made another one.

After Pippa's first year of college, Mattie sold the house. She paid off the mortgage and the back taxes and put enough aside for Pippa's last three years of school. Just before she moved to Portland, Mattie split the proceeds fifty-fifty, money that Pippa had mostly spent. She gave Pippa exactly half of everything else, six spoons, six knives, six forks. Fifty books. One of the two big tables. Pippa put her things into storage and sold them before she moved to Hilo.

In the late afternoon after dumping the cuttings into the compost pile, Pippa headed downtown. She had her dinner menus down pat: tofu and broccoli, red curry over basmati, salmon on mixed greens, mushroom rice. Repeat. Breakfast was always yogurt, fruit, and granola. Lunch was nuts and half a papaya squirted with lime or some leftovers from the night before. All the clerks at the KTA knew her, nodding or giving her the half-smile for a resident but not a true local. The store aisles were clumped with retired mainlanders, all of them sun-damaged and wearing inappropriate shorts.

They smiled at Pippa as if in collusion, and she smiled back, hoping to get by without conversation. In the produce section, she hovered over the vegetables, nodding to Brian, who worked most afternoons.

"Just put out some new broccoli." He pointed to the fresh, densely headed stalks. "Get it while you can."

During her first shopping trips here, Brian seemed to flirt with her, despite the fact he was a true local. Maybe Dale from meats had flirted, too, but while she tried to figure out how to respond, they stopped. Now they made pleasant conversation, the same way they did with the retired folks.

"Watch out for the condiment aisle. Some kind of medical emergency."

"What?" she asked, but Brian was rolling away with his trolley.

Pippa put a head of broccoli in her wagon and then headed past the packaged meat toward the aisle in question. Three emergency-garbed men stood with hands on their hips staring at something. Wildly reflective even in the daylight, their bright greens, yellows, and reds beat into Pippa's head. One talked into a radio giving an update. A man, chest pains. Maybe diabetic.

"I need some soy sauce," an older woman said to a KTA employee. "I really, really need it."

"You can't go down there yet," he told her.

"Well." The woman looked at Pippa for agreement, and when she didn't get any, she huffed past.

Pippa stared, though she could see very little. The only visible body part was the man's outstretched arm on the painted concrete floor, his skin weathered and dark, fingernails thick and slightly yellowed. He was tented by highly trained professionals, their gear spread around them. The radio crackled again, and then came the clack of the gurney being wheeled down the aisle.

"Step back," one of the emergency workers said, and Pippa did, literally backward. One step, two. How she remembered that feeling of being saved. Her body on the flat expanse of a gurney, the air on her face as they pulled her up.

"I said step back," the man said again, even though Pippa was moving away. But he knew. He saw that in her mind, she was standing right next to the man, urging him to be okay. She was next to him as they rushed to the hospital. She would be hovering all night, until it was over.

The next day, Pippa logged off work at the same time there was an earthquake in Papua New Guinea. As she closed her computer, her phone buzzed with texts, the island chain of Hawaii under tsunami alert, even though the forecasters predicted a non-event. Worse than the imagined tsunami was the rain that started to fall, hard, the roof clattering. Wind slapped the house and blew palm fronds onto the sodden grass.

She didn't bother to shutter the windows but sat the kitchen table, watching as things fly past, the view as it had been that last day with Em. All they had been able to do was look up, still and quiet.

"That looks like an ice cream cone," Em had said about a cloud. "Maybe a dog."

"Or a cat," Pippa had said, trying to encourage Em to say more. But mostly, Pippa had stared at the back of Em's head, her hair dark and wet.

Pippa's cell phone buzzed and then at the same moment, the house phone rang, a sound she'd only heard a few times because no one ever called it.

"Hello?" she said into the home phone. Her cell phone blared *Mattie*, and then went to voice mail. Her sister kept alerts on her phone, and this call was likely about the tsunami and the storm, a double whammy.

Her cell phone rang again. Still Mattie.

"Pippa Randall?"

"Who is this?" Perhaps she was being evacuated, Pippa thought, the threat finally real once again.

"My name is Donald McDonald. I represent the estate of Nathaniel Brower."

"Estate?"

Donald McDonald cleared his throat. "You haven't received our letters?"

Pippa sat down on the kitchen chair, blinking into the refrigerator's stainless door.

"No."

"I'm sorry to say that Nathaniel Brower died last week."

Pippa's mouth opened, and she stopped breathing for a moment. Outside, the world crashed against Nathaniel Brower's home. All the trees threw what they could at his former house. Her former house. Soon real estate agents would converge. The furniture would be sold; the yard would be wacked into an inch of its life. The tenant would be evicted, she that tenant.

"Miss Randall?"

"I'm sorry," she blurted, a strange, ragged feeling in her throat.

"My apologies," Donald McDonald said. "You should have received notification by now."

She wanted to tell Donald that no one even knew her enough to notify her about anything, much less news about Nate's gentlemanly farm. His mail was forwarded to Santa Fe; she had a box at the post office. She was a stranger who talked with him once or twice a month. She did what he asked, but he didn't know anything about her.

"I'm calling because I have news. It's good, I hope."

A wall of wind beat the kitchen window like the whirring whap of helicopter blades rising out of a canyon.

"What do you mean?"

"Mr. Brower left you the Hilo house."

The kitchen light wavered but stayed on. Pippa wiped her eyes and nose and looked out the window, expecting to see a giant wave cupping the shore, but all she saw were clouds.

"I don't understand."

Donald cleared his throat, discomfort in the gravelly sound. "Mr. Brower had no remaining family or beneficiaries. The rest is going to various charities. I'll be sending a letter he also left for you."

Pippa brushed tears off her face with the back of her hand. "Wait! How—how did he die?"

"I'll send the letter," Donald said. "And expect some registered mail with important documents. Also, I've contacted a Hilo lawyer who will help you with some documents. She'll be in touch."

She gave him her PO Box address. "Thank you," Pippa said, wishing she could really say that to Nate. She pictured walking up to him and giving him a hug, but she didn't even know what he looked like, having only seen a few photos in the house. Maybe he'd looked like the sound of his voice. Skinny, light, full of hope.

By the time Pippa got on her flight to Hilo, it had been years since she'd been in the air. She wasn't afraid until the moment she sat down in her seat, economy, 29C, an aisle seat close to the bathroom. As the flight attendant went over lifejacket protocol during a water crash, the cabin began to swim with orbs of light. Pippa's entire body felt ready to split from her skin.

"Are you okay?" the college kid next to her asked.

"Sure," Pippa said as she dug in her purse.

"I'm Malcolm," he said, extending a hand. But Pippa was opening a pill bottle and swallowing two of the Trazodone she'd been prescribed years before.

The rest of the flight was a dark wall of nothing. When she woke up, she was in a dorm at the U of H with Malcolm and his two nervous roommates. Her luggage was in the middle of the room like a lonely piece of Stonehenge.

"They were going to arrest you for drunk and disorderly behavior," he told Pippa when he drove her up to Nate's. "I had to tell them that you were my sister. I lied and said you had the flu."

Pippa wanted to invite Malcolm into Nate's house, she didn't. At first, she thought she'd call him, but she didn't do that either. When she went into town, she almost hoped she'd run into him, so she could take him for a drink or a coffee. But she never saw him, not once. By now, he must have graduated and gone off into his real life, the kind that other people seemed to take for granted.

Pua Kalawaiʻa's law office was on Laukapu Street, not too far from Big Island Candies, a store Pippa went to when she sent her guilty gift basket to Mattie every Christmas.

Pua's receptionist had bright red lips and heavy eyeliner, as if preparing to join Cirque du Soleil. Her body was tight like the piece of corded rope that she might twirl up.

"Ms. Kalawaiʻa will see you now." Her voice was like flung knives.

Pua came out of her office and gestured Pippa in. She wore no makeup and a very sensible lightweight blue suit and black flats. She was round where the receptionist was thin, but Ms. Kalawaiʻa was sturdy and buttoned-down.

"Pua Kalawaiʻa," she said, reaching out a hand.

"Pippa." Pippa put her hand into Pua's, shaking in a way that she hoped meant business.

"Sort of like the lottery, right?"

Pippa sat down on the chair, as Pua riffled through the pages of the document. "Wish someone left me a big house when I was twenty-five."

"I—"

"So lucky."

Pippa's thighs tightened, her feet solid on the floor. She could call Donald McDonald and tell him to get another lawyer.

"This Mr. Brower. You know him well?"

"I've been taking care of his house for three years." Pippa rubbed her right thumb, her skin dry, her cuticles ragged from all the gardening.

"So like I said." Pua handed over a document with a yellow tab showing Pippa where to sign. "Lucky duck."

"I'm not lucky." Pippa scratched out her name once and then again.

Pua waited for more and then when Pippa just stared back, she said, "Lots of people don't have their own house."

Pippa nodded. "I know."

As Pua waited, Pippa flushed, heat filling her from the top down.

"So the deed has been transferred," Pua said finally. "And these—Grace, I need the next page notarized."

Grace came in with her box and pens and stamp. "Driver's license."

Pippa swallowed and pulled out her ID and handed it to Grace who began to fill in a form. This was almost over.

"Do you know how he died?" Pippa asked.

Pua and Grace both looked up from their papers.

"No one told me," Pippa explained.

"Suicide," Pua said. "Apparently he was really sick. Oh, and here. I was supposed to mail this, but you're here. He wrote this to you before, well, he did it."

Pippa took the envelope, and then she signed everything

Grace and Pua asked her to, leaving her thumbprints behind as proof.

It hadn't rained for months, so when it finally started to pour in mid-December, everyone was ecstatic. But who expected the oils to pull up from the roads? No one, apparently. And really, who cared when everyone could finally turn off their sprinklers and lawns could grow back? Trees and shrubs plumped up and dust washed off cars, buildings, and benches in dirty rivulets.

Each morning, Pippa had a long, uphill walk to the bus stop, so on Day Four of the deluge, Em told her enough was enough. Mattie had already left for her English comp class at the college, so this seemed the best plan. "You are showing up to school like a wet rat. Let's go."

Pippa hadn't been paying much attention. She was reading a book and then looking at her cell phone, hoping her best friend Julia would call. She worried about smashing her orange in her backpack. Em turned on NPR, so she wasn't talking, either. It wasn't until she said, "Oh, no," that Pippa looked up into a world that was off balance and then spinning.

It was slow at first. The car sliding diagonally down Honey Hill Road, surfing the asphalt sideways, gaining speed, bumping up and over the curb and the partially broken guardrail and then hurtling down, down, down into the canyon below. The dry years killed the Monterey pines that might have caught them, but the car crashed through branches crisped and sharpened by drought, one busting through the windshield to impale Em on their way down. They smashed, they spun, they flew, finally caught and pulled back by an enormous eucalyptus.

For a few seconds, they hung, bouncing, ready to break free and fall to the road far below. Too afraid to cry, Pippa looked at Em who was unconscious, part of a branch in her stomach, one of her arms at a strange angle.

"Mom," Pippa whispered, scared her voice might add weight to the car.

The rain beat down, drops heavy like bullets. Pippa watched her mother, noticing a new wound with each breath: ear, shoulder, forehead.

Pippa was untouched, snug in her seatbelt cage, her side of the windshield unbroken.

"Mom," she whispered again, and then again, one "Mom" every few seconds until finally Em woke up.

"Oh," she said. "Pippa. Are you okay?"

"I think so," Pippa said. "But…."

Em passed out again, coming to every once in a while to reassure Pippa that someone would come and save them. Somehow, the invasive, improper eucalyptus kept them aloft, even when the wind whipped lashes of rain against and then into the car through the broken window.

"Mom," Pippa kept repeating. "Please."

Not only did Pippa get the house, a yearly operating budget, the land, and all of Nate's possessions in the Hilo property, she got his car, too, the Honda she'd been driving since she moved in. When she got home from Pua's office, Pippa allowed herself—for the first time—to go into Nate's room. He'd taken most of his clothes and personal things during his move to Santa Fe, but he had a dozen or so Hawaiian shirts in the closet and flip-flops lined up underneath them. There were sculptures of Hawaiian birds and a few prints of the ocean and the volcano in a sulfurous uproar, but nothing else offered up much information.

On his dresser, there was a photo from a long time ago, the edges yellowed, a smiling man in a uniform, Naval, maybe. Pippa had only seen Nate in photos in the kitchen drawer, but she thought she saw a resemblance. His grandfather. After opening a few drawers and surveying the shelves, Pippa couldn't find any other evidence of family, a fact that both lawyers had confirmed. Nate had ended up alone in the world except for Pippa who lived thousands of miles away, a total stranger.

In the dining room, Pippa sat at the table and opened the letter. For a second, she thought she might recognize the handwriting, but of course that was ridiculous. Nate had never sent checks, but paid all bills online. He emailed and texted but never wrote, so she was surprised by his light and flowing scrawl.

Dear Pippa—

Sorry to do this in such a terrible manner. I didn't tell you I was sick when you applied for the job. Hilo didn't have the medical services I needed, so thus the move to a city with a specialist. It wasn't the art that drew me to Santa Fe, but the art was nice, at least for a while.

After our first phone conversation, I looked you up. A background check with a couple of services. You were going to be taking over my life, after all. I didn't mention it later because nothing bad surfaced. Then one service sent me some links about you and your mother, but what happened wasn't something I could work in when discussing the roofing materials or patching the driveway.

What a horrible story. So much danger. You were there for her until she wasn't. After I read the articles, I wondered how you still managed to walk the planet, much less move to another state and set up a whole new life.

You took such good care of my house, and by extension, me. Thank you for giving me something so special—the ability to not worry about all that while I worried about my health.

But things aren't going well, and I'm done. Flat out ready. It's been a long haul. I'm not scared. And I don't want you to feel responsible for any of this. You did everything right, and even if you'd known, you couldn't have changed my mind.

Quit that remote job. Enjoy the house and the farm. You know exactly what to do—you've been doing it for three years. Buy a couple of goats. What about one of those miniature donkeys? Plant some tomatoes.

All best,

Nate

Pippa sat at the table. The sun set and the bullfrogs started in with their nightly honking. Her mother was next to her, nodding as she read the paper. She smelled like toast and sleep and black tea. On the stove top, something odd, lentils with squash or bouillabaisse. Sunflowers in a vase on the pine table. A book, a magazine, and a newspaper. As she read, Em pushed her hair back and chuckled at something she read, looking up at Pippa and then reading aloud.

"So funny," Em said, slapping her hand on the table. "Who would have known?"

Pippa could only stare. Em. Her mother. Mom. Blonde-haired and brown-eyed, just like Mattie and Pippa. Slightly crooked nose. Fingernails painted pink, her favorite color. Mattie now was exactly as their mother had been for all their childhood.

Just before Pippa had heard the helicopter and saw the helmeted man dangling outside her window, her mother died. Pippa hadn't really known clinically, but something heavy lifted from the broken cab.

"Ten more minutes and that branch would have snapped," she'd heard a firefighter say in the hospital hallway. "Can't believe it held that long."

The last time she saw her mother, Pippa was in the air, held flat in a metal gurney being lifted into the sky. Despite being strapped down and buffeted by the great machine above her, she turned her body so that she could see her mother's hair, part of her face, her hand. Later, her throat raw, she would remember she had been screaming.

The helicopter pulled her up and up, her mother a dot in a giant tree.

Outside, the rain stopped. Pippa flipped on an outdoor light, terrifying a gecko, who stared at her with its bulging dark eyes, all parts of him pulsing with fear. His green, blue, and red sides heaved air in and out so fast Pippa worried he might explode.

"Sorry," she whispered, stepping back. "No one expects the Spanish Inquisition."

The gecko opened his mouth, and Pippa waited for a second to see what he might say. Instead, he licked his left eye. So she turned toward the lush darkness. From the trees came the popping whoop of coqui frogs, another interloper, calling and responding to things she could only begin to guess at. A warm wind held her upper arms and face. In the distance, the ocean tumbled against the invisible shore.

Pippa waited. Sucked tight to the wall, the gecko's breathing finally slowed, his rhythm like the wind. In and out, in and out. After a moment, he started to amble up the wall, one sticky foot at a time.

Monsters in the Agapanthus

My niece clutches the kitchen doorjamb, her brown eyes wide. Her face is streaked—mud, dirt, ash. Her hair is flyaway, thin, uncombed. "I saw from the window. There's monsters in the bushes."

I put a dirty breakfast bowl in the dishwasher, wipe my hands. She's a dark child, full of nightmares. I wish I weren't taking care of her. "What bushes?"

"The shiny ones. At the bottom of the backyard."

"The agapanthus." I snap the door shut, cutlery rattling. "There are monsters in the agapanthus."

Deena nods. She's so slight, so tiny, I see her swallow articulated in her throat. I'm not sure what a seven-year-old should weigh, but it's got to be more than this, her arms like reeds, knees like tangerines, eyes that take in the entire world.

"Come on," I say, holding out my hand, dried and chapped from so much handwashing. "I'll show you the monsters."

The monsters rattle the agapanthus, moaning and growling like something from a sci-fi movie. In the cheesy film, the small things would spring out, covered in fur or scales but certainly with enormous teeth, biting one of the supporting cast. Deena shudders at my side as the tuberous mounds shake, the growls roaring to a crescendo.

Deena grabs my pants. I imagine her on a ship, the stowaway clinging to the sail during a sudden squall.

"Puppies," I say. And just then, Marcel and Lulu pop out, Lulu first, and she tears off to the far side of the yard, Marcel at her heels. They are smaller than the noises they make but fast and very happy.

"Puppies?" Deena gasps.

"More fur tornado than monsters. My friend calls them a furnado," I say, but Deena, rapt, walks toward the puppies wrestling in the far corner of the yard. I follow. Her sad sneakers are flat and worn. A tag sticks up from her small t-shirt.

"I didn't know you had puppies," she said as she crouches down, her hand hovering over Lulu's head.

"I didn't know I had you till last night," I want to say but don't. Instead, I say, "Twelve weeks old. Got them almost half a month ago."

"Are they nice?"

"They have sharp teeth. But they don't bite hard."

Lulu stops her tussle, pants, looks at Deena, and then moves into Deena's cupped palm. Lulu licks her, snuggles against Deena's stick body, and then reaches up and licks her face. If Lulu were a cat, she'd be purring.

That's when Deena finally cries.

I don't know how to make food kids like. Mostly, I make what I want, and no one but me likes to live on bowls of fruit and yogurt. Or vegetables and hummus. Smoothies made of brown bananas, rice milk, and ice cubes. Everything served cold. So I tried to remember something my mother used to make us, her repertoire Midwest and bland. I settled on mac and cheese. And carrots. I know kids like carrots, the kind that don't look like roots but severed thumbs. For dessert, I bought some popsicles, but the minute I left the store, I remembered you can make your own with orange juice.

The fork is enormous in Deena's hand. There's a snail's trail streak of snot on her right cheek, but I don't say anything. She's not paying attention to her meal but to the puppies and my adult dogs, all slumped like sacks at her bare feet. That's how I used to sit at the dinner table. After my mother died, no one was there to make us wash before meals. We were raised by ourselves and neighbors. By wolves, my older sister Mara used to say, Mara who escaped the wolves. But maybe that's why I like dogs so much. They remind me of home.

"They have long tongues," Deena says, chewing. She's missing a couple of bottom teeth, and I hope that's normal.

"The better to lick you with." I glance to see if she gets the reference, but she keeps eating.

"Are they the babies of your other dogs?"

I chew the slightly too *al dente* macaroni and then swallow. "I got Rocky and Bullwinkle a while back. But they're all pound pups. Saw them advertised in the paper and went and got them."

Deena blinks and then nods. "You've got a lot of dogs."

My friends have said the same thing, most telling me I'm becoming the crazy dog lady. They threatened to stage an intervention.

"A puppy is like two dogs," I say to Deena. "So that means I don't have four—"

"Six!" Deena cries out.

"That's right," I say, oddly proud. "For about a year that's what it will feel like around here. Six dogs."

Deena watches me, and I can see her calculating how her time and this new dog time will mesh. She chews her food and then says, "You can buy six leashes and six bowls."

"And six beds," I say. "We can have a doggie bunk bed."

"A doggie hotel!"

She looks as if she will say something else, ready to add more detail to our doggie world. But then she catches her breath, almost sinking down onto her chair, shrinking back to her true shape. Then it's my turn to cry. Or at least feel like it. Only seven, and she knows how not to believe in hope.

My youngest sister Lynn, Deena's mother, is the pretty one. Younger by ten years and spun of darkness and bright blue and long leanness, she came wired for excitement. None of us three older siblings liked her much. She was the last evidence of our parents' connection, something we'd given up on years before she was born. But after my father disappeared and before our mother died, Lynn was the designated favorite, given all the treats we'd been trying to discover for years. By the time I left for college, I'd decided Lynn would either be a stripper or a dentist. All those big white teeth.

Deena clacks her fork against her bowl, spearing a raft of macaroni. After every two bites or so, she leans down to pat one of the dogs, Rocky licking her hand and wrist. I idly wonder about worms and other parasites but then decide to ignore the thought because the attention makes her smile. Besides, by the time the symptoms of either appear, Deena will likely be somewhere else.

"My mom never let us have a dog. Said they were too—something. Something that ends with a y."

"Hmmm," I say, thinking of Lynn "Y" words. Sexy, crazy, naughty, scary. Lynn took her time getting to neither dentistry nor sex work. Instead, she became the girl next to one powerful man after another. Well, if the married president of a lawn mower company or owner of a string of auto-body shops counts as power. Which one ended up Deena's father, I never knew. But at some point just shy of forty, she got pregnant. Of course, she was the best looking pregnant woman ever. Glowing, lush-haired, still slim-hipped, she carried Deena as if born to breed, like one of those native women who pushed out her baby over a dirt-floored hut and then headed back to the harvest. It was just plain irritating.

My other siblings and I strung together rosaries of questions, all starting with *What, How, Why, Where.* Lynn never answered a one of them, disappearing sometime in her third-trimester and sending only yearly shots of her baby girl.

"Can I have some more?" she asks. My heart flickers as I scoop out a mound of mac and cheese.

"What next?" my girlfriend Sal asks me.

"Don't know. Some lawyer will tell me, I'm sure."

I slump against my headboard, staring out into the hallway and the half-open door of the guest room where Deena sleeps. When I was little, I thought every night was a horror show. Something was bound to get me. Monster, ghoul, vampire, devil.

I'm waiting for Deena's scream.

"I guess I can't come over for awhile."

I sigh. It's possible Deena is an answer to my prayers. Sal and I have needed to break up for months. She wants to travel the world, and I just want to stay home. She turns up the heater, and I'm in favor of blowing out the pilot light. On and on. Who knows what she would think of Deena.

"Let her settle in," I say. "Give her time before we tell her that the wombat she's living with is not only a wombat but an old grizzled lesbian."

"You're hardly grizzled." Sal laughs. "Well, maybe in some places."

"She's been through too much," I say. "All she needs is more oddness."

"Nothing gay is odd in California, you know. Deena's got to know that, too."

"She's not happy," I say.

"Why isn't she with your brother? The one with the kids."

"Hardly kids. They're in college."

"But still," Sal says. "There's got to be a bicycle or a ball hanging around. A twin bed."

"Oh," I say, standing up. "She's calling for me. I'll call you tomorrow."

"An—"

But I hang up. The house is silent, except for the hum of the furnace, set at 68 degrees.

"Marcel and Bullwinkle fight a lot," Deena says. Today it looks as though Deena's been playing with someone's lipstick, something I haven't worn since 1976. Back then, it was called lip gloss.

"It's a male thing. They're establishing who's boss."

"Who is the boss?" Deena bites down on another strawberry and watches Marcel mount Bullwinkle's left leg.

"That we don't know yet." I hand Deena a napkin.

"I think Marcel." She watches them play. "He's smart. He knows when you're going to feed them before anybody."

"He hears me thinking about dog kibble."

"He hears you think about walking to the kitchen."

I laugh. "He is smart, then."

Deena puts down her bowl of berries and wanders out onto the lawn where the dogs tussle. I've heard a lot of things in my life, too, and none of them very good. I'd like to unhear a few dozen for sure. The way a foot in a shoe on a floor trying not to make a sound sounds. The way a hand on a blanket sounds. The way cries-that-aren't-yet-cries sound. No one should hear things that aren't hearable.

All at once, I hear the things Lynn must have heard. The whack of air right by her head. The crack of skull on the tile. Breath leaves my body, air leaves the backyard. How I want to reach out and save her the way I never did when she was alive.

"Maybe Lulu's the boss," Deena says. "She's smart, too. And she's the cutest."

Like Lynn, I think. It's the cute ones that go first.

The social worker is a stereotype, though why we call things that are true and real a type, I don't know. She's soft and formless, and her glasses rest on the bridge of her nose. Her gray hair is *bone fide* grizzled, but full, a messy halo. Her bag could be Mary Poppins', a carpetbag full of magic. Except, of course, she's here on business. My brother Tom picked up Deena for a park and ice cream afternoon, and I'm left to answer the questions.

"She was brought here two nights ago." Mrs. Rossner reads from her notes. "A friend of the mother's dropped her off?"

I nod. "It was late. I was half asleep. Didn't ask what I should have."

"The next morning is when you found out." Mrs. Rossner peers up over her glasses. "That's when you got the call."

I look down at my feet in their sensible gardening shoes, one shoelace puppy shredded. The night Deena arrived, I'd spent a few hours disgusted with Lynn for her this and that, her wastrel-ness, her incapacity, her inability to see that her shine had dimmed. Couldn't she grow up and take care of her child? I thought every bad thing I could and lined up some more to mull over in the morning. Then I'd paced the floor, emailed my siblings and Sal, worried about how I could keep the child alive.

"Right," I say. "The police came here. One of Lynn's neighbors called it in."

"This happened the night your sister's friend dropped Deena off?" Mrs. Rossner says gently. "And the friend did it?"

I nod. "They think so. It's ongoing."

Mrs. Rossner shakes her head as she writes. "Does Deena know?"

"No," I say.

She looks at me, bites her lip, shrugs. "You've got to tell her soon. Otherwise, she'll be upset about the wrong things."

Hadn't I known this my entire life? I'm the poster girl for being upset about the wrong things, *Who Else Can I Blame* my *cri de couer*.

"I was just waiting. . ."

"She'll blame her mother for this."

And why not? Isn't it Lynn's fault, all of it? She put herself right in the middle of bad and stayed there. That friend of hers, the one at my doorstep with Deena in the middle of the night. I could see why Lynn hitched her star to his. I can't totally fault her. Even as I stood there in my terrible bathrobe, bleary-eyed, and foul-breathed, I saw his smile. The way he cocked his head. The tattoo on his bicep.

"Worse, she'll blame herself." Mrs. Rossner rummages in her bag. She pulls out pamphlets and papers. "There are support groups."

"There's not going to be time for support." Whatever help Deena needs will come from the place she lands. Here? I can be all popsicles and puppies. Mrs. Rossner looks up, her black eyes intense over her eyeglasses.

"You *are* going to keep her with you?" She leans forward, close enough I can see the soft dark hair on her upper lip. She smells like gingersnaps, like the witch in *Hansel and Gretel*, the one who charmed with sweets.

"I—"

"After what she's been through?" Mrs. Rossner flips through the file, thicker than I'd ever imagined it could be. Seven years old!

"I'm not cut out for this."

She rolls her eyes. "No one's cut out for this. Who could be? Not a pattern anyone wants to repeat. Middle of the night and all with no warning. But she's your niece. She needs something known right now."

"But later—"

"One day at a time," Mrs. Rossner hands over the information. "Make that one minute at a time. Or less, if need be. Just do it."

Tom's wife brought over real food, and tonight, Deena and I dine on lasagna. As she scoops up noodles and sauce, I study her head. She doesn't remind me of Lynn much, not with her sparse hair and plaintive features. That was one thing Lynn never was. She never complained. Not when we were eating lentils for weeks or her shoes fell apart. No, Lynn found a way to get invited to live with the Robinsons down the street. We'd see her through the window eating chicken drumsticks and drinking Coke, as if she'd been put into the wrong family the first time. Found at last. She even convinced them to send food to us, leftovers and junk food we ate in a tear.

"When's my mom coming?" Deena's fork clatters to the table. Rocky whines, the puppies stir.

I look down at my plate, a massacre of red, a swirl of blobby cheese. "When did you last see her?"

"I already told the men that." Deena's voice is dime hard.

"Maybe so, but I didn't hear."

She sighs, her thin shoulders touching the back of her chair. She's sitting on an old phonebook and Shakespeare's collected plays. Her eyes are caverns I could get lost in—the entrance frightening, the way out impossible.

"She put me to bed. Then Bobby woke me up."

"How did he seem?"

For a second, she looks right at me and then shrugs.

"You didn't see anything. . .her again that night?"

Deena shakes her head and then leans down to pet one creature or another. One time when I was parking near the ATM, I noticed a big white truck in the space next to me, red and black words spelling out "Crime Scene Cleanup." I waited in my car for awhile, just to get a gander of the person who would perform the services listed on the truck door: *Homicide, Suicide, and Accidental Death Remediation: Cleaning, disinfecting, and removal of all contaminated items to restore the scene to a safe, non-biohazardous state.*

Whoever hosed down the gibbets never showed up. But I had the picture. I got it. The brain matter on the wall. The pools of blood. The trail the dying person left as she clawed her way to the backdoor, trying to get to her car, forgetting about her child even as she died. Then the body, lifeless, stiffening, fingers permanently clutching the carpet.

The puppies growl and tumble. Deena smiles.

"Ice cream?" I ask.

My parents were young and stupid when they got together, and stupid stuck. Here I am, a mostly retired physical therapist, working one or two days a week at the local convalescent facility. Stroke patients. Surgery rehab. I live in Oakland as quietly as I work. No permanent relationship to my name other than four dogs and a handful of family. We keep our distance, circle the holidays as if they will explode on contact. Then we sit in chairs as if dressed in bomb suits, immobile, muffled, hot as hell.

What else? Oh, Sal in the corner, still waiting. Deena asleep in her bed, only a few years away from the acting out that has to happen sometime. Memories, too. Guilt, boatloads of that. And monsters, still, at night, in the closet, under the bed. The old monsters I brought with me from my childhood. Now they live in the agapanthus with Deena's.

The months click into summer. There's a short session at the local elementary school with a reading focus. Testing. Counseling. A tutor. Tom's wife arranges play dates when I have to work. My friends bring over toys. Deena has her first physical. I go to support meetings and learn about "Talking About Violence" and "Talking About Death." I hear stories that remind me of my own. And Deena's. I come home and make things that are hot. Chicken coated in flour and baked in the oven. Boiled green beans from a neighbor's garden. Sticky potatoes riddled with lumps but full of butter.

I break up with Sal, who is surprisingly calm. Later, I hear she'd already found another girlfriend and was hoping to let me down easy. Win-win, as my mother used to say when someone handed her a drink.

The puppies grow, the days lengthen, August heat pulses up from the ground. Deena and I sit outside on the bench after planting nasturtium seeds. Wisps of fog roll in from San Francisco.

Marcel and Lulu race their superhighway through the agapanthus, but they've grown—gaining a pound a week—and their fighting seems real, though so far, no bloodshed. Rocky and Bullwinkle lie on the grass, waiting for calm. Deena has gained weight, too, though she still looks like she might fly away on a stiff wind.

"Your mother," I begin. "The night you came here."

"I heard it." Deena stares out at the agapanthus. "She screamed."

"What did you do?" I breathe out.

"I waited. There were other noises. And then Bobby came and got me. He put a blindfold on me. Told me it was a game. Hide from Mommy. He put me in his car, and we drove away."

Something tears at my throat, and I cough. "Did he tell you what happened?"

"He said my mom didn't love him. Or me. He said he knew how to make things better. That he was going to take me where I'd be safer."

I only met Bobby the once, at the door. There he was, half murderer, half savior. "Do you feel safe here?"

Deena nods.

"Could you live here?"

Deena is silent, her eyes trained on the puppies' path. A figure-eight, an X, a back and forth. Around and through, over and under, their growl and whine and moan rising and falling. They break free of the plants and then dive in again, their every move, lunge, and parry hidden under the dark green of the agapanthus, the leaves shiny, roots deep.

I Would See Everything

I am standing in a long line at the last video store in America waiting to pay for the movie my two sons finally agreed to rent. It is 7 o'clock on our first Friday night in this town—Walnut Creek, though we have not seen one walnut tree—and Max and Alex have picked out a slasher movie. I stare at the movie case, flipping it in my hand. The actor on the cover seems to have been whipped or burned terribly, his bald head and fleshy face a mound of sinewy scars, yet he is leering at me. Usually when the boys want to rent a movie like this, I launch into a sociological discussion of violence and America's sick view of teenagers, but I was too tired tonight, so now I wait in line. The woman behind me pulls newspapers and coupons out of her large purse and bumps into my back rhythmically.

I want to ignore her, but she says, "Oh, sorry," her breath smelling of green beans and bacon.

I feel my face falling slowly downward; my skin, my lips, my makeup. I shuffle slowly forward on the tattered red carpet.

"Hi. Are you a member?" the young man asks when I finally reach the counter. I look up at him, but I can't make it to his eyes. I watch his smooth chin with its sparse dark beard. Every hair seems to be the same length, straight and separate on his soft skin. I think he is smiling.

"I've never been here before."

His chin shakes, and he rubs a hand down a long black shank of hair.

"You've got to fill in this form before you can rent anything. Here." He gently hands me the form and a pen. "You can stand over here while you do it."

I meet his eyes finally, and he is smiling. "That's a really scary movie, you know," he says, pointing to the case, and then my boys, who at six and nine were clearly too young for such horror.

"I'm pretty scary tonight," I say, moving my purse and application over to the other side of the counter.

I have not felt this incapable since my high school physiology teacher made me dissect a twenty-pound feral cat by myself. I sat at the black Formica table, staring at the prone, formaldehyde-pickled cat, finally sobbing when my teacher handed me the huge silver shears to cut the rib cage. The bones snapped like wet twigs.

"Are you done?" the young man asks.

I hand him my form. "I guess so."

He looks at my form carefully and then types my information into the computer. A whiz of noise, and then a card pops out of a printer. He hands it to me. "Make sure you have this when you want a DVD."

As he takes my money, I notice that he does everything purposefully. The money goes into the register just so; the pen fits right above the cash register keys. His arms are as smooth as his chin with the same sparse hair. He wears three thin bracelets made from colored yarn on his wrist, and they slip down to his hand and up to his mid-arm as he works.

I look at his name tag: Tran. "Well, Tran, thanks a lot."

He looks away from me as Max and Alex run towards the counter. He looks back to me and raises his left eyebrow. "Have a good time."

It is Saturday afternoon. Max and Alex got tired of unpacking boxes, so I found the address of a public pool, and now I am sitting on a chaise lounge at Heather Farms watching Alex swim. Max is sitting on the chaise next to me, a snorkel in his mouth.

"I'm pretending to be Freddie," he says, breathing loud snorts through the tube. Before we moved, Max insisted on having his head shaved. He used to have a flat top, like Arnold Schwarzenegger, but he wanted to go one step further, to have that G.I. Joe look. One day, my mother pulled me aside and told me that her bridge group was concerned about Max.

"They wanted to know about his chemotherapy. They thought he had leukemia," she said. Later, as Max, Alex, and I moved boxes into our new house, I wondered if this was the same reason my neighbors gave us such pitying looks.

Up until he was three, Max's hair was long and curled at the ends like those fancy twist straws. Every day, someone would ask me about my beautiful girl, pointing at Max as he ran, his dark hair bouncing on his shoulders. I finally took him to the Supercuts downtown where Max told the hairdresser he wanted to look like the Terminator.

"I'll be back," he said into the mirror at the finished product, the distressed hairdresser looking on.

Now, his scalp shimmering under what remains of his hair, he breathes into the snorkel awhile and then takes it out of his mouth. "If there was a bomb, would I be able to survive with this snorkel?"

He looks at me anxiously, his brown eyes wide, his body tense.

"What made you ask that?"

"With bombs there's lots of smoke. No one can breathe."

"I don't think there will be any bomb, Max. But if there were, the plastic might melt on your face. Best to learn to breathe without it."

Max holds up the snorkel and shakes his head. "The snorkel would survive! I could breathe anywhere." He puts the snorkel back on and begins to walk around the pool towards Alex. Alex follows his brother with his eyes, and then thrusts his body up in the water and shrugs.

When Simon was alive, he would read to Max out of a big *Time-Life* book, stopping to detail the aircraft carriers, U-boats, and fighters. When they reached the chapter on Hiroshima, Simon would talk about the loss of human life. There were pictures of nuclear shadows, the etched remains of the people who died in the first second of the explosion. One man had just climbed down a ladder and hung up his belt, the surprise in his body registering in black on the concrete wall. A little girl had just thrown a ball in the air, her outstretched arms the testament of her joy, her shadow the record of her life. Max would nod solemnly as Simon reassured him. He told Max that we learned our lesson. Sometimes Max would ask "Dad, will someone bomb us?" And Simon would reassure him again, talk about disarmament, lulling Max with words that went over his head. Just the sound of his father's patient voice was enough.

After Alex is done swimming, we decide to go home. There are so many boxes to unpack, so much I need to go through. Before we left Sacramento, my mother, in desperation, took all of Simon's clothes that I had stubbornly left hanging in the closet for months and gave them to Goodwill. She wanted to do something for me before we moved. When I told her and my father that I was moving, had found a new job, had bought a new house, they both sat at their kitchen table staring at me with eyes I can only describe as mournful.

"But Dana, you shouldn't move to escape. You need your roots," my mother said, putting a strong hand on my knee. "And the boys!"

I had thought of these arguments for months. I was running away from my troubles. I was yanking Max and Alex from the only life they knew. But living in the house with Simon—his scent still on the comforter, his golf clubs in the basement, his mail showing up every day—was killing me. And there were things I was not ready to see now with fresh eyes: the vase he bought in Guadalajara, his tennis racket, his high school graduation photo. The first time I saw the picture, we were visiting his mother's house on a spring break during our last year of college, and he pulled out the frame from the closet.

"Who is *that*?" I asked interested, the young man's long black curls and bronze face sexy despite the late seventies' black bow tie and wide-lapelled jacket.

Simon looked at me astonished, then irritated. "Me. Of course."

"Are you jealous of yourself?" I asked, pushing him softly on the arm.

From then on, *Who is that?* became our joke phrase for anyone attractive. And when we were married and in our first apartment, I put the picture on the mantle. *Who is that?* I would whisper in his ear at night, biting his thick, brown butter lobe.

I remember the smell of Simon's neck and the thickness of his ear, and I turn to Alex as I drive, realizing I don't want to go home just yet. "Let's go get another movie. And a pizza."

Alex looks wary. "But we want to watch the one we got last night again. It's good."

"Let's get one we can all watch, okay? Then we can eat pizza and unpack at the same time."

Alex looks at me, calm and sad. Everything about Alex now is quiet; even his chlorine blonde hair seems to be more of a fading than a bleaching. At night, I go into his room and pet his head, his hair flat against my palm. Somehow, I want to give him life again, like when he was born or when I breastfed him. He was such a round, fat baby. My mother-in-law still talks about the ripples in his thighs. But there is nothing I can give him now to nourish him, to plump him to a rosy, rippled, smiling baby. When Simon died, Alex fell into the background, into the quiet questions he had that no one could answer. Instead of talking, he started to watch us. If I were arguing with Max, Alex would appear as a silent referee. I was worried, so I took him to a therapist. After a few visits, the therapist asked me to a session alone.

"Alex misses his father, and he needs to be sad. It is healthy for him to be sad now. He isn't depressed. He is grieving." She stopped talking and then looked at me. "Have you grieved yet?"

I was too busy to grieve but every second was grief, the kind that pulled on the corners of my mouth all day, constant, dark, and heavy like an implacable sinus infection. I went home that early afternoon and cried for it all: for Simon being hit by a drunk teenager in a two-and-a-half ton muscle car; for his life being over when there should have been so much more left; for me being alone with two boys; for my fear of being in charge, responsible, an adult; for my desire, sometimes, to not do any of it at all, to leave these two grieving children and my own hollow sadness as if they were horrible movies.

But aside from keeping Simon's clothes hanging like thin ghosts in the closet, I did do it all. I emptied the safety deposit box the morning after the accident because my father was worried about probate. I met with the boys' school teachers, telling them both about Simon; telling one about Alex not talking; telling the other about Max's obsessions. I tried to explain that one child would probably blow-up the first grade, while the other would fade so far into the fifth that no one would find him. I filed the police report and then listened to the teary sixteen-year-old talk about how sorry he was to the judge, his parents ashen and stiff behind him. Despite wanting to fling myself over chairs and tables and people and kill him with my hands, I wanted to hold him in my arms and weep for us all, Simon's death changing all our lives.

I kept getting up every morning, making breakfast, driving to school and to work, helping with homework. I kept moving, but my sternum seemed to freeze up and petrify. When I breathed in, pain fell down my ribs like stairs.

I could still smell my husband on my blankets and hear his voice on the answering machine, and I could imagine his strong body flying over our Camry, flipping in the air, and landing on the wet street. I could see him lying, just moments dead, his last breath somewhere still in the room, his eyes blackened, his head swollen and bloody, his dark skin as white as the hospital sheets. I looked at his naked body, so perfect, and wondered how death really worked. How did the body just shut off? How did blood stop flowing? Nothing my physiology teacher taught me—not even my own cutting of the cat's stiff flesh—had prepared me for this.

His body might have been dead, but everything else between us had never been so alive. I saw him in the kitchen plates, the tools in the basement, the curve of the iron's handle. His hands still held everything except me.

For months, each night I would think about my last look at him. As I walked out of the hospital room, I turned back and saw that his hand curled over the edge of the bed, as if he were hanging on, as if he could push himself up.

I carried this picture around with me the same way I carried around Max's and Alex's school pictures in my wallet. I wondered when I would finally go crazy, sink into total depression, or become violent. I found it hard to believe that I was functioning. It was only a matter of time before I put towels under the kitchen door and stuck my head in the oven. But I didn't go insane and I kept not going insane; I started thinking I could live through this and that is when I decided to move. As I drove the U-Haul down

Interstate 80, Alex and Max alert and silent next to me, I finally comforted myself by imagining myself the most well-adjusted insane person I had ever known. In that instant, every normal thing I had done since Simon died seemed miraculous.

My hands are on the steering wheel at three and nine, the safest way to drive. Alex reaches over and pats my right hand. "Okay, Mom. But let's go home and get the other movie first."

Max pulls on my seat from the back, the snorkel still in his hand. "I want to get one about the war."

Alex turns to him. "We are going to get one we all like."

Max slams into the back seat. "I'm not going to watch it. I'd rather drown in *Thompson's Water Seal.* I want one about war." He puts the snorkel in his mouth and snorts.

Alex looks forward and says, "It'll be fine."

Max finally sighs noisily through his snorkel, then spits it out. "Mom, what would happen if I had eyes all over my body?"

Alex and I laugh. "I don't really know, Max. It would be interesting."

"It would be great," says Max. "I would see everything."

Tran is working again tonight, and he smiles at us as we walk in. He is watching a video, and I realize it is one of those movies made from an E.M. Forster novel. The soundtrack reels with violins and harps, and Tran is counting money.

"Hi, again," I say.

"So, Freddie scared you too much?" he asks, shaking his long hair back.

"Not me," says Max. "I would shoot him with my machine gun." Max holds his snorkel vertically and makes shooting noises so violently spit drops to the floor. Alex shrugs again and then pulls his brother toward the back of the store.

"You can see we are a non-violent family," I say, embarrassed. I walk over to the stacks. I fumble at a movie, wondering what I am looking for.

Tran comes up behind me. "You know, we just got a couple of good movies in. Let me show your kids." I look into his eyes and stop breathing for a second. There is an answer in his voice, something I have been listening for. His left eyebrow lifts like a quiet exclamation on his forehead, and whatever he is saying, I want to believe him. Now it seems so easy to just hand someone my boys for a minute, the same way the doctors handed them to me when they were born. I let air slowly out my mouth and find my chest feels lighter, like I can breathe without a snorkel.

Tran pats my arm quickly; so fast, that when I look down, his hand is back on his hip. "Hey, guys," he shouts. "Come over here. I've got some movies for you."

My boys follow him towards a stack of videos under a sign that reads *New Releases*. Alex laughs as Tran points to a movie. Max pokes a movie down with his snorkel; Tran picks it up and hits him gently on the head. The three of them move slowly down the aisle. In my mind, I pick up Simon's hand and uncurl it from its grip on the bed. I kiss each finger before I lay his hand on his smooth chest. I walk out of the room.

I hear Max and Alex laugh, the room suddenly grows light. I have been lifted above my boys, both graceful and alive in their bodies. I can see everything in this minute, even the walnut trees on green hills, the nuts black and smelling like rain.

Acknowledgments

The following stories first appeared, in slightly different forms and often under different titles, in the below journals. I thank the editors and assistants who worked with me on each.

Your Impossible Voice: "Trick of the Porch Light"
Press 53: "Escape Room"
Pithead Chapel: "Murder House"
Story Quarterly: "What Glory Chose"
TINGE Magazine: "The Brightness of Things"
Buffalo Almanack: "A Miracle, Really"
Edge: "Shortcut Through the Alley"
Carve: "The Possibility of Fire"
Devil's Lake: "That Strip of Earth"
Sou'wester: "Accepted Forms of Ruin"
Palaver Journal: "The Happiness"
Mason's Road: "Don't Forget About Me"
The Worchester Review: "The Dry Years"
Lunch Ticket: "Monsters in the Agapanthus"
Fine Print: "I Would See Everything"

The above list represents thirty years of writing short stories and to thank everyone who taught me fiction, touched these stories, counseled me wisely and well would take more pages than are appropriate. I've been lucky enough to take many wonderful classes, attend fantastic lectures, and sit at the feet of the benevolent and wonderful—so to all whose thoughts and advice I've reached up and grabbed, many thanks.

I am so grateful to Maria Maloney and the Mouthfeel family for bringing this collection to the light. Thanks, too, to my first fiction teacher Anne Lamott who, many years ago in a bookstore in Marin, wrote, "You are the real deal" on top of her xeroxed copy of "I Would See Everything." Thank you Anne for believing in my story and my writing and giving me that first big shove. Thanks to Scott Nadelson, who is the most dedicated (and flat-out smart) teacher I've ever had and who was consistently beyond generous with his feedback and time. Josh Mohr read so many of these stories and was more than supportive. David Borofka and Lisa Cron at UCLA Extension lent so much of their expertise to my stabs at the short story. Pam Houston dug right in and provided great counsel. Thanks also to Donna Miscolta and Joan Frank for their kind words about this collection.

Then there are the writing friends, dear friends, thoughtful readers who have given their time and brilliance to these stories: Kris Whorton, Mishele Maron, Julie Roemer, Darien Gee, Warren Read, Lexi Pandell, Sarah Phipps, Karen Ekstrom. Thanks also to my writing groups, especially to Judy Myers, Maureen O'Leary, Joan Kresich, Keri Delaney-Gregor, and Gail Offen-Brown for thoughts over the years. Thanks Ann Pancake, Rick Barot, and other members of the RWW family for support.

Finally, thanks to my family, my sons Mitchell and Julien, my husband Michael, my mother Carole for being the people I was graced to have around me in this lifetime, all of us here through thick and thin, better and worse, now and later.

About the Author

Jessica Barksdale Inclán's fifteenth novel, *The Play's the Thing*, and second poetry collection, *Grim Honey*, were both published Spring 2021. Her novel, *What the Moon Did*, was released in February 2023. A multiple Pushcart Prize and Best-of-the-Net nominee in poetry, fiction, and nonfiction, her work has appeared in or is forthcoming in the *North American Review*, *StoryQuarterly*, *Salt Hill Journal*, and *Tar River Poetry*. Her work has been recognized and honored by *The Sewanee Review, The Wigleaf* and *The Ocotillo Review*

Recently retired, she taught at Diablo Valley College in Pleasant Hill, California for thirty-two years and continues to teach novel writing online for UCLA Extension and in the online MFA program for Southern New Hampshire University. She lives in the Pacific Northwest with her husband.